Also by Jasmine Black

Taken by Two Sugar Daddies
Taken by Two X-Husbands
Taken by Two Elves

The Pleasure Collection
Pleasured by Her Guards
Shared

Standalone
Shared Boxed Set

Pleasured By Her Guards

A Three Book Collection
Jasmine Black
These naughty guards truly misbehave...

Taken by Two Prison Guards
Jasmine Black

Twenty-three-year-old Madeline "Mad" Madison has quite the temper. She got ten years to life in prison due to her getting mad at her late boyfriend and there's only one way she knows of to keep herself calm and she's not getting *that* type of rehabilitation in prison. That is, until she's assigned hard labor and taken by two naughty prison guards.

Taken by Two Lifeguards
Jasmine Black

TWENTY-TWO-YEAR-OLD professional swimmer and Olympic hopeful, Katie White, goes to the beach every day to continue work on her training by swimming in the ocean...and to do some secret naughty stuff on the side.

She also loves the lifeguard eye candy. Skimpy swim trunks on tanned muscular bodies put her in a really good mood. But the

1

lifeguards don't seem to know she exists, especially after she broke up with her lifeguard boyfriend, Chad.

When Katie suddenly gets caught in a malicious storm, two lifeguards come to her rescue. One of them is Chad!

Stranded in the first-aid shack and being almost dead has made Katie awfully cold and her two lifeguard rescuers are going to warm Katie up nice and slow...

Taken by Three Bodyguards
Jasmine Black

TWENTY-ONE-YEAR-OLD Stephanie Stephenson has been in a safehouse with her three sexy bodyguards for many months. She's a lone witness to a murder and they've been protecting her from Santonio, the mob boss, who has vowed revenge if she dared to testify. It's all been strictly professional and platonic with her hunky bodyguards. Now the trial is over and Stephanie is free to go.

But her three bodyguards have other plans for Stephanie...very naughty plans.

Other stories by Jasmine Black include:

Taken by Two Doctors, Taken by Three Doctors, Taken by Two Bikers, Taken by Three Bikers, Taken by Two Billionaires, Taken by Three Billionaires, Taken by Two Bosses, Taken by Two Cowboys, Taken by Three Cowboys, Taken by Two Firefighters, Taken by Two Carpenters, Taken by Two Personal Trainers, Taken by Two Santas, Taken by Two Elves, Taken by Three Bodyguards, Taken by Two Cops, Taken by Two Prison Guards, Taken by Two Lifeguards, Taken by Two Mountain Men and more!

Copyright

Author Note

This is a work of fiction. Characters, places, settings, and events presented in this book are purely of the author's imagination and bear no resemblance to any actual person, living or dead or to any actual events, places, and/or settings.

Taken by Two Prison Guards

Jasmine Black

Twenty-three-year-old Madeline "Mad" Madison has quite the temper. She got ten to life in prison due to her getting mad at her late boyfriend and there's only one way she knows of to keep herself calm and she's not getting *that* type of rehabilitation in prison. That is, until she's assigned hard labor and taken by two naughty prison guards.

Copyright

Author Note

This is a work of fiction. Characters, places, settings, and events presented in this book are purely of the author's imagination and bear no resemblance to any actual person, living or dead or to any actual events, places, and/or settings.

Chapter One

"Hey, Mad. Get your ass out here! You're on the chain gang today."

Wow! I couldn't believe what I was hearing. I'd applied for work on the chain gang months ago and I was finally in!

Quickly I stepped to my prison cell door, which was all shiny gray metal and I slid my hands out the slot so he could shackle my wrists.

I'd been in solitary confinement for a month because once again my temper had gotten me into trouble, but I just couldn't keep calm when my rights were being trampled on, especially when it came to food.

I'd demanded my fair share of vegetables that particular day and when I was told they were out of vegetables, I'd lost it on the bitch behind me in the line up who'd told me to get over it and get a move on. I'd put her in the infirmary with a broken nose and a concussion. Too bad I had to learn the hard way there were no rights in here for prisoners, even for the ones, like me, who took no shit from anyone.

"You're in for some hard labor, Mad. Heard talk that you'll be raking leaves out of the ditches all day," Officer Myers said as he looked through the small bullet proof Peeping Tom window at me. He had short cropped red hair with matching freckles and pimples, along with a smirk on his face, but that didn't bother me much. I didn't care about hard labor. I just wanted to get out of this freaking isolation, the penitentiary and into the fresh air, even if it was to work my ass off.

My cell door slid open and he instructed me to walk ahead of him down the hall. We passed through several units, each one having locked doors that slid open when Officer Myers spoke into his breast mike. And then he directed me into a small room where seven other lady inmates were seated along a wall on a bench.

All of them looked mean and pissed off when they saw me walk in. I didn't recognize any of them. They must be from the other Blocks. So I just ignored them.

Besides, they were ugly older bitches and I didn't know why they were all frowning. They should be grateful to get to the other side of that twenty-foot-high cinder block wall topped with razor barbed wire.

"Okay ladies, there are your boots and gloves. Get those orange jumpsuits on over your clothes. Pick what fits you the best. Leave your shit on those shelves over there. After you're done, line up here for your leg shackles." A bored looking bald guy said from the other side of an open doorway.

He was pointing to a really long shelf lined with folded orange suits, work boots and gloves and then he pointed to another shelf that was a quarter full of other people's shoes. I figured those shoes belonged to ladies from other chain gangs that had already gone out this morning.

The women grumbled as we all stood and headed to the shelves. I removed my shoes, slipped into a jumpsuit that fit relatively well, then tried on a couple of pairs of boots until I found a comfortable size then put them on. I grabbed a tattered soft pair of work gloves and joined the other ladies in the line. I was at the end of the line, but I didn't care. I was getting the hell out of here for the day.

Had I thought I'd be doing hard time in a freaking prison for killing my boyfriend, I would have simply made myself disappear before I'd accidentally, or maybe not so accidentally, killed him.

But hey, in my opinion, the women of the world were better off without that piece of shit. I clamped down on my anger at thinking about him and watched as the guard handed me shackles for my ankles. I put them on, the clinking sounds of the heavy chains on my wrists and now my ankles irritated me.

Oh great. I couldn't even pick my nose without the chains making a racket. And so much for trying to make a run for it.

"Don't look so fucking down, prisoner. You're pretty enough. I'm sure you'll come back all smiles, especially on your first day." The old bitch of about fifty, who stood in front of me, muttered over her shoulder as she frowned and stared me up and down.

"Fuck off," I whispered.

She chuckled. "You're a live one, aren't you. The guards like the rowdy young girls. They'll have some fun with you."

It was my turn to frown as I wondered what she meant by her remarks.

The clinking of everyone's chains grated on my nerves as we were ushered down a hall into a large garage containing many prison vehicles and then we were guided onto a waiting prison van.

But I forced myself to stay calm and gaze out the window as the van started to move out of the garage and into the sunny day.

Five years I'd been here. Five years since I'd been in a vehicle.

Fuck, it was great feeling the sunshine beating on my face as it streamed past the thick-paned windows. I closed my eyes and remembered how I'd gotten here.

It had been a sunny autumn morning just like this one. I had once again been hoovered back into resuming a relationship with my on again, off again, boyfriend, Dane, who kept dumping me and then coming back.

During our time together, he'd gone from Mr. Jekyll to Mr. Hyde and back to Mr. Jekyll again. He'd been like a freaking seesaw and I never knew what mood he'd be in from one minute to the next. I'd get red-hot angry at him for his behavior and he'd say let's have sex to calm you down. So we did and I'd always feel better after a good roll in the hay.

As the relationship progressed he'd started blaming me for all his wrongdoings. Accusing me of sleeping around yet I found out he was the one screwing around. Then he'd started hitting me and then he'd blame me saying I had forced him to do it because of *my* anger.

Over the months I'd known him, he'd broken my jaw, my arms, ribs, fingers, and I couldn't name it all. To this day, healed body parts still ached.

Every time he left me; he'd come back a changed man. Romancing me with dates at expensive restaurants and professing his eternal love to me and that he was a changed man because of me. For some crazy insane reason I thought this last time he would stay Mr. Nice guy.

I was wrong. Again.

We'd had great sex that last night together, to "calm me down" because I'd been so angry at him for leaving in the first place. We always had great sex but I had come to realize over the years of incarceration, that's all we'd had.

Every other thing about him was no good. He'd been a virus that had tapped into my abandonment issues, he'd screwed with my head and used me for a place to stay and of course for sex.

When I had first met him, I'd ignored that gut instinct telling me he was all wrong for me. But he had love bombed me right at the beginning, wining and dining me, bringing me flowers and telling me everything I'd wanted to hear. That he'd loved me at first sight. I'd been on cloud nine, feeling like this was the man of my dreams. He'd been perfect. Or so I'd thought.

He told me he'd never hurt me like my last boyfriend had done. Rex had ghosted me, breaking off our relationship without so much as a reason. Dane said he'd never abandon me like my father had done when I was a kid. On and on he'd gone with his fake promises.

Instead of listening to my gut instinct and insist we take it slow and that I shouldn't be answering all of his prying questions so soon, I'd thought he was seriously interested in me. I'd swallowed his I love you bullshit hook, line and sinker and I'd let him into my heart and into my bed way too soon. He'd bedded me on our second date and had moved into my apartment within a week of us meeting at a bar.

Before I knew it, he'd begun to control me and isolate me from my family and friends. He'd come up with all kinds of excuses of why the two of us should be spending the evening together in bed having great sex instead of my going to my mom's birthday party or a friend's baby shower or whatever was going on that particular night.

Or he would conveniently get sick when I was supposed to go on a weekend getaway with my girlfriends. Or he'd harp on about how he couldn't stand my little sister and preferred it if the two of us go on a trip together conveniently every time Donna would be in town visiting my mom and wanted to swing by and see me too.

It had happened so slowly, this controlling and isolation, that I hadn't realized how bad it had gotten until I was hooked on him to the point I was terrified to break it off.

Finally I'd connected in my head that something was really wrong when I'd accidentally dropped my cell phone into the toilet at work where I was a receptionist for an electronics company. Of course, the phone had been fried. I'd been in such a panic, rushing to the office landline phone to call him asking his permission to go for a shit so he knew where I was in case I missed a phone call or a text from him asking what I was doing.

But I'd let my fears slide because I didn't want to displease him. Didn't want him to abandon me.

But he'd done it anyway. He'd begun ghosting me. Disappearing for days on end. Of course, that triggered my abandonment issues, making me try even harder to please him every time he came back from who knows where.

Yeah I was so hooked into that toxic bastard's abuse, it wasn't even funny.

Unfortunately for me, that addiction to him had been my downfall.

Chapter Two

That sunny autumn morning, after a wild night of make-up sex, which had calmed me right down, as it always did, he'd said he was leaving me for some other woman. Again.

I'd been so hurt and desperate and angry. We'd stood in the apartment hallway as I'd literally screamed I would kill him if he left me.

As he tried to go down the stairs, I'd grabbed his arm.

He'd laughed in my face; told me I was a stupid cow for ever believing that he loved me and then he yanked his arm free. He'd lost his balance, fell down a flight of stairs and broke his neck.

I'd heard the crack, ominous and loud. I can still hear that crack sometimes when I have nightmares about it.

Someone called the cops. Neighbors told them I'd been screaming, shouting, and threatening to kill him. One of them said she'd seen me push him down the stairs. Maybe from her angle, that's what she'd thought. Later I learned he'd been fucking that woman behind my back and that he'd told her I was a crazy woman.

So yeah, because of her testimony I wasn't a hundred percent sure I hadn't pushed him. I might have. It had happened so fast. A shitty pro bono lawyer had gotten me aggravated manslaughter and I'd landed in prison doing ten to who knew how long.

Shit happens, was the last thing my sister said when we'd hugged goodbye before I'd come out here. I'd told her not to visit and to go on with her life and not look back.

She hadn't visited and not once did I hear from her but I was glad she'd gone on with her life.

But my mom wrote letters and sent pictures. Donna was now married to some nice guy who worked as a taxi driver and they had two little girls with another girl on the way.

But then mom had up and died on me. Some rare brain cancer. A friend had written me a letter to let me know that within two weeks of her diagnosis, she was gone. No funeral due to the Covid pandemic. So yeah, shit happens.

As so many other times over the last years, I found myself thinking my life would have been so different had the apartment building elevators not been out of order that day, he wouldn't have taken the stairs and life would have been so much better had I never met the skunk.

I must have dozed off in the lure of the warm sunshine because when the van hit an exceptionally big bump, I opened my eyes to find we were in the countryside now. Huge towering trees lined both sides of the gravel road on which we were travelling. Bright yellow, orange and crimson red leaves were swirling down like a colorful snowstorm as the wind blew against the tree branches.

The scenery was really pretty.

I smiled. Probably for the first time in five years.

I watched as we passed a chain gang. The women were wearing bright orange jumpsuits just like the ones we wore. They were raking leaves in deep ditches. They didn't look happy. Not one of them looked up, nor did anyone wave.

Beyond the trees and ditches, farmland stretched out everywhere. Some pastures were filled with golden bales of hay and other pastures had fluttering yellowing corn stalks or bright orange pumpkins splayed out upon the ground.

The driver of the van turned off the gravel road and kept driving along a rutted trail that had seen better days.

Up ahead was another vehicle. A white van similar to this one, with the words of our prison on it.

"Oh look, the welcoming committee is here." That same woman who'd spoken to me earlier muttered from the seat behind me.

She didn't sound cheerful.

"They must have gotten word there's fresh flesh in this gang. They're gonna try her out," replied an older woman sitting on the bench seat across the aisle from me.

She turned to look at me and my tummy dipped like I was on a roller coaster.

"Aren't you the lucky one," she said in a low tone.

She suddenly smiled at me and wiggled her white eyebrows. She only had one tooth in her mouth and she looked like a creepy old witch.

Man, I hoped I didn't look like her when I got that old.

The van stopped. The door opened.

"Alright, Madeline Madison. You get out here. The rest of you ladies stay seated. You'll be coming with me."

There were a couple of snickers from the women and then silence.

I swallowed as uneasiness whipped through me.

I was to go out there with those two prison guards? On my own?

Reluctantly I stood and peered out the window trying to see where the chain gang might be out here in the middle of nowhere. I saw nothing but a large field filled with orange pumpkins and the two male prison guards standing by their vehicle.

"Come on, Mad! Get a move on! Daylight is burning!" the van driver shouted. He sounded irritated.

My chains clinked like crazy as I hobbled down the aisle of the van. All the ladies were as quiet as church mice and looked the other way as I passed them. They all wore frowns. Kind of like they were pissed off.

Oh my gosh! Was I getting preferential treatment because it was my first day? Were they jealous?

I shook my head at that crazy idea.

My uneasiness vanished when I stepped out of the van and felt the crisp cool October air whipping against my face.

I was free. Well, sort of.

I held my breath as I stood there and sized up the two prison guards.

They wore identical uniforms. Dark blue shirts and tan pants. Shiny black boots, and dark blue baseball style hats with the words Prison Guards emblazoned in white lettering across the front. The two men were cute and well built. Wide shoulders. Slender hips and long legs.

Something hummed to life inside of me when I spied bold erections pressing against their pants.

But they wore lots of weapons.

Each man wore what I called a beating stick. They each had a holstered gun on their belt too. There was mace, tasers, handcuffs and walkie talkies.

These guys looked like serious business. Once again the thought of escaping seemed out of the question.

When I looked up into the faces of the two tall prison guards, alarm bells went off, but in a really enjoyable way. Each guard had a predatory look in his eyes and I sensed I was their sexual prey. I wasn't sure at the moment if I might just be fantasizing, but my pussy was clenching and creaming hot liquid like it hadn't done in quite a few years and my nipples suddenly seemed bigger as they pressed against my bra, aching to be free.

Suddenly I got the feeling this wasn't going to be a regular day of hard labour, at least not in the traditional chain gang sense.

I blew out a tense breath as the van filled with my fellow inmates drove away.

"Good morning, officers," I said politely.

Just because they owned me here in the prison system didn't mean I had to be a bitch. Besides, I always found you get more of what you want if you blow honey at the guards. And I just wanted to be outside of the prison as much as possible and for as long as possible.

"Morning, "the tallest guard answered. He held a clipboard in his big hands.

"Just want to confirm you are Madeline Madison. In for aggravated manslaughter, ten years to life."

He looked up from his clipboard awaiting my answer.

I realized he had the most fabulous aqua blue eyes when the sun shone on them.

I nodded.

"I'm Officer Dixon and my partner is Officer Ashton. You're here to pick pumpkins. Follow us."

I found myself relaxing. For a few seconds there I'd fantasized about a menage a trois with these two men.

Bummer. I'd much rather be having red hot sex instead of picking freaking pumpkins.

Be careful what you wish for, a wary inner voice warned. I shrugged it off. Yeah, right, like in my wildest dreams.

I followed the two guards into a dense line of trees, fully expecting to find a gang of women working on the other side, but there was no one around. Just a field loaded with big fat orange pumpkins.

It kind of reminded me of the story of Cinderella and for a split second I wished I were her and one of those pumpkins would magically turn into a beautiful carriage and whisk me away from here to some faraway land and to my very own Prince Charming.

"Here. Use this to cut the stems." Officer Ashton broke into my fantasy.

He held out a utility knife and stood back as I took it. He had dark brown eyes and dark brown hair with a tiny ponytail that peeked out from the back of his hat.

He pointed down the field.

"Over there is the line of bins for you. Fill each one level to the top, then go to the next bin."

I spied a long line of wood slat bins. Had to be at least fifty of those containers and just one of me.

Lovely. It appeared I wasn't going to have an easy first day as I'd hoped a few minutes ago.

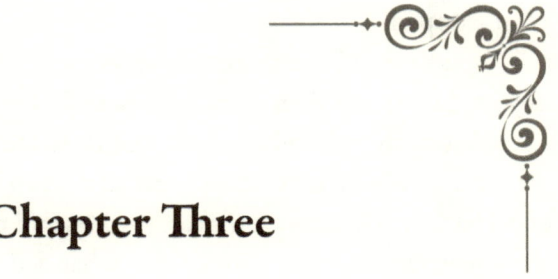

Chapter Three

I headed toward the nearest pumpkin, crouched, sliced into the stem, picked up the heavy orange fruit or vegetable or whatever the hell it was and walked to the bin.

"Handle them like eggs, please," Officer Dixon instructed. He held a pen to the clipboard and watched me.

"Or gently like a man's balls," the other officer chuckled.

I bent over, rolled my eyes at his comment and placed the pumpkin into the bin.

If these two officers had balls as big as these pumpkins they'd be in the field helping me and I was sure they wouldn't help because from my experience the guards were like ornaments. Standing around and looking pretty.

And so it went. The two guards watched me work from afar, studying me like I was some insect and I kind of ignored them. I was too busy slicing into pumpkin stems, breathing in the fresh air and languishing beneath the hot sun.

After awhile though, my shoulders were getting sore. So was my back, my thighs and my neck. The chains were rubbing my wrists and ankles something awful. I was also really getting hot being trapped in this orange jumpsuit, not to mention I was getting thirsty. But I knew it would be rough the first few days. Especially since I'd been lounging around like a prison princess the last five years.

So, I just ignored my owies and kept going until I heard a sharp whistle.

I stopped.

"Break time! Your box cutter stays there. Show me your movements as you place it and then come over here!" One of them shouted.

Cautiously I placed the cutter on the edge of the bin.

Like seriously here. They were armed to the teeth with weapons and I had chains on my wrists and ankles and they were afraid of me?

I reached the men. One of them handed me a nice big paper cup filled with ice cold water. I drank it like there was no tomorrow and I wished for another one. I wasn't offered seconds so I kept my mouth shut.

"Do you need to relieve yourself?" Officer cute blue eyes asked.

"No, sir."

"Sit down here on the ground. Relax, prisoner," he instructed.

I sat where he pointed. The ground was full of leaves, but damp and cold. Again, I said nothing as the wetness seeped against my behind.

"You've got a fifteen-minute break," Officer Dixon said.

I nodded and stared off into the distance watching a bunch of black crows circling around up in the sky. They were probably waiting me to drop dead and then start picking at my corpse while these two guards just stood around like the glorified decorations they were and watched.

I chuckled aloud at that thought, unable to stop myself.

"Something funny, Mad?" Officer Ashton asked.

"No, sir."

Officer Dixon was looking at his clipboard as he hovered over me.

"Your records show that you appear to be a very good prisoner. You have no problem following orders, except for some hiccups along the way due to your short temper. It seems to get you into trouble."

Just sticking up for myself, asshole. But I didn't dare say that aloud. He would think I was having an attitude and write me up.

"Yes, sir."

"Have you tried the anger management courses?" Ashton asked.

"Yes, sir."

"Not working from the latest solitary run, eh?" he asked.

"No, sir." I wished they would just shut the hell up. I wanted to listen to the wind rustling through the branches and pretend I was somewhere in a park or something.

"You appear to follow instructions easy enough this morning. Lots of girls would have already broke down and complained about something like a sore back, wanting out of their jumpsuits and chains or wanting to go back to the prison. But we can see that you're one of the tough girls," Officer Dixon complimented.

"I try, sir." For a brief moment, I felt proud. That is, until his next question.

"Aside from your temper, are you a submissive?"

I blinked as shock rolled over me. Had I just heard right? The prison guard had asked me if I was a submissive? Like in sexual terms?

I kept my eyes locked straight ahead, realizing that my first instinct about their predatory gazes and those erections had been correct. Now I understood the comments back on the van from those women. I was a lucky one, one of them had said. They must know what goes on out here. How come I hadn't heard about it?

"You're not answering my question. Are you a submissive?" Dixon asked again.

I swallowed at my suddenly dry throat. My heart was picking up speed and to my surprise, my pussy was quivering and growing hot.

"I'm not sure what you mean, sir?" I said tightly and kept my gaze on the circling crows in the field.

"Let me rephrase this. If we give you an extra fifteen-minute break, will you let us suckle your breasts?"

Heat fused through me at lightning speed. I began to tremble, in a really enjoyable way, as his words sank in.

Did they have a suckling fetish?

The idea of having two men's hungry mouths at my nipples hadn't even entered my mind. I inhaled deeply and took a moment to compose myself. I was a pretty fast thinker and I needed to spin this to my advantage.

"If you give me those extra fifteen minutes as alone time before you suckle at my breasts, then sure. But no bites and no hickeys," I said as I stared straight up at them. No way was I going to be having to explain myself in the shower room to the other women or to the nurse in the infirmary with infected bites on my breasts.

Both men grinned down at me, their faces transforming from seriousness to glee.

I had no problem noticing their erections were much bigger pressing against their pants now.

"Do you have trust issues?" Officer Dixon asked with a snicker.

"Let's just say I like to get paid ahead of time." I answered.

I was really getting tense. What if they decided to make a report on me if I didn't comply? I mean, I wouldn't mind having a little sexual fun and call me totally freaking insane, but the idea of these two men at my breasts was turning me on big time.

Huh, maybe I was the one with a suckling fetish?

"Just so we understand each other. What happens out here, doesn't get told back at the prison. It stays here." Officer Ashton's gaze had returned to one of seriousness again.

Like whom was I going to tell? I was a loner in the prison system and that was probably why I'd never heard of what went on out here. Up until today I'd just wanted to do my time and get the hell out.

"I understand," I said.

Both of them swore softly, and to my surprise, they walked away, leaving me alone. I blew out a nervous breath. What in the world had I been thinking agreeing to this?

Why was I feeling so flushed and so unbelievably aroused? Even my ass was getting in on the action, clenching up a storm as I envisioned one of them sliding his shaft into my anal canal.

Wow, over five years without sex sure did wreak havoc on me. At this point I was ready to say yes to anything they asked, even if it meant having them screwing my brains out in the field while those crows watched us. Anything so I didn't have to lift another heavy pumpkin.

So instead of having an enjoyable break, my imagination went wild as I waited for the two men to return. The break seemed endless, torturous.

Instinctively I knew they were just testing out the waters, so to speak, to see how compliant I might be. Or if I would run hysterically back to the prison crying rape.

By the time they returned, I was wound up so tight, I could barely think straight.

"Time's up," Officer Dixon said in a guttural voice.

"Have you changed your mind?" Officer Ashton asked. His voice was husky yet alert.

I shook my head.

"Good. Then stand," Ashton ordered.

I did as he instructed and stood in front of both of them. I noticed they'd removed their hats and their weapons were no longer on their belts.

Okay, this was interesting. No one had weapons, but still, there was two of them against one of me. And I had the chains hobbling my legs and wrists.

To my shock, Ashton produced a key.

"Unlock your wrist chains. I don't know about you, but the sound of those chains is grating on my nerves," he said.

"Try being in my shoes," I muttered.

I took the key.

I jammed the key into the wrist restraint. It popped open and the chains dropped onto the ground.

I wondered how he'd had the right key for my chains. Had this all been planned ahead of time? It surely seemed so.

Wow, it felt good to have my arms free from the heaviness of the metal. I handed him back the key and he shoved it into a breast pocket.

"Now unzip your jumper and let's get a nice closeup look at your breasts," came Officer Dixon's instruction.

Chapter Four

I guess I didn't move fast enough because he repeated himself.

"Unzip your jumper," Dixon said again.

I could see the heat flaring in the two men's eyes. Could feel an insane need to do their bidding. Maybe I *was* a submissive? I had never thought of myself as one, but maybe that's why I had been so easily duped into getting into bed with men in my past?

"If you insist," I said in as soft a voice as I could muster.

Unexpected excitement roared through me as the men watched my every move. I reached up and found my zipper, then slowly, ever so slowly, I pulled it down to my waist and smiled inwardly.

I was wearing a T-shirt underneath.

Disappointment flared in their eyes.

"Off with everything above your waist just like we agreed," Officer Ashton whispered.

"And no more games," Dixon said in a serious tone.

Hmm, had I frustrated them so easily? Having such power over these two prison guards was irresistibly amusing.

"I'm not sure what you mean," I teased.

I'd never been one to be embarrassed at being naked in front of a man. I'd always been comfortable in my own skin and being out of the prison walls, it almost felt like being free. I even felt playful.

"We are in charge. When we instruct you to do something, you will not play sexy. Is that understood?" Dixon growled.

Oh crap. For a moment, I *had* felt freedom sifting through me. Despite his warning, my mind was beginning to imagine all kinds of scenarios of getting them to do my bidding. But it appeared they wanted to remain in charge. At least for now.

My hands trembled as I slid my arms out of the jumpsuit. I couldn't resist continuing my slowness and I made sure to keep my movements seductive.

My mind was whirling with plans. If I could get these two men hooked on me, then I might be able to get more out of this than a mere extra fifteen-minute break.

I reached for the hem of my T-shirt, watching them carefully. Their eyes followed my every move with captive interest. The two men were truly thrilled, and so I lifted my shirt up and over my head. The only thing left was my bra.

"Go on," Officer Ashton prodded.

Both men had moved closer and stood directly in front of me.

I began to remove my bra, feeling both disbelief and some weird, electrified anticipation. My pussy was wet and I noticed their faces were flushing.

Suddenly, my swollen breasts spilled free and I stood tensely as the two guards stared.

"Wow, they were right. You do have magnificent big breasts. So juicy looking," Officer Dixon commented.

I stiffened. Okay, so who was *they*? His comment solidified my suspicions that this had all been set up. "Look at those luscious ruby red nipples," Ashton said.

"Like big red lollipops," the other replied.

Sexual arousal coursed through me at the intoxicating way these two men were ogling me. Desire raged in their eyes and I could literally see the tension tightening their bodies. Could feel the tension zipping through the air and wrapping around me.

"Just stand nice and still. No touching us under any circumstances," Officer Ashton whispered.

I gasped in surprise as both of them moved at the same time. They reached out, their hot hands quickly cupping my breasts. I cried out as their heads lowered and their heated mouths covered my nipples.

Their lips tugged on my sensitive flesh. Their tongues licked and lapped. Instinctively I arched my back, pushing my breasts harder against them needing a firmer contact.

I loved what they were doing to me. Understood at some primal level that this was a seduction.

My nipples grew hard and achy as they forcefully sucked. Intense heat fused throughout my body.

"One day we may even decide to make you pregnant, so we can get our daily intake of milk. Would you like that?" Dixon murmured around my quivering nipple and then took it right into his hot mouth again.

I couldn't believe what I was hearing and to my surprise a powerful surge of desire roared through me. I creamed at the thought of being pregnant. My belly swollen. My breasts heavy and ripe with milk for them to suckle.

Oh have mercy, the idea of it was turning me on so bad. I must have gone nuts in the prison system for such a suggestion to excite me. I'd never wanted kids. But now, suddenly, I did and I didn't even know these two men!

I watched them beneath dazed, half-lidded eyes as they sucked harder, their mouths tugging and bruising my tender nipples. The pulling created sensations that spiraled to my belly and then arrowed down between my thighs. My pussy felt heavy, hot and throbbed with need. The need to be taken by these two strangers.

I moaned, whimpered, and cried out as their large hands massaged my breasts and their hot lips forcibly tugged on my straining nipples. I was seriously creaming up a storm. My lower belly was tightening. My pussy was clenching. My breathing became fast.

A powerful surge of arousal lashed me as I imagined the two men sliding their cocks into me.

I swear I was about to orgasm. And then I *was* orgasming!

I shuddered within the uncontrollable spasms and moaned as my tender pussy muscles clenched on empty air. I became lost in ecstasy. Bucking and keening at the beautiful onslaught of convulsions.

Pleasure lashed through me like electrified whips. I knew I'd want more of this when it was over.

But all too soon my orgasm ebbed, leaving me panting as the two men drew their mouths away.

"Don't read too much into what I said about getting you pregnant. It was just in the heat of the moment," Dixon whispered. But from the lust shining in his eyes, I knew he was lying. I knew he had some sort of breast and lactating fetish.

I nodded jerkily.

For a few luxurious moments, I'd dreamed his craziness. And it was crazy. But pretending and play acting didn't hurt anyone.

"Break time is over. Back to work. Leave your breasts free for us to see and we'll keep your wrist restraints off, deal?" Dixon asked.

He was back to his serious attitude again.

I could protest. Hell, I should protest. At the very least I should bargain for some longer breaks if they wanted to see my breasts some more.

But I'd just had a damn good climax and I felt satiated. I wasn't in the mood for anything but following orders. Yet I seriously couldn't wait to see what else they wanted from me.

I adjusted my prison-issue jumper by securing the top part around my waist, tying the arms together and then I returned to working with the pumpkins, topless. I just loved having my wrists freed from the chains and having my breasts exposed to the fresh air and sunshine. My nipples ached from the prison guards forceful lips but I had the added bonus of them ogling me.

They couldn't get enough of watching me and I couldn't wait for them to suggest doing some other sexual activity with me. But I also realized I had to have patience. I didn't want to come across as desperate and that I actually craved more. If I did that, I'd lose the ability of bartering with them.

So, I waited for them to make their next move.

Lunch came and the guards presented me with the traditional prison food. Boring tasting sandwiches bottled water and a fruit cocktail in a small tin. I also noticed their weapons were back on their belts.

To my angst, they left me alone to eat, moving away down the treeline where I noticed they ate delicious looking extra large submarine sandwiches and steaming coffee from a Thermos.

They also remained serious for the rest of the day, standing or sitting like ornaments on the empty bins as they continued to watch me working topless. My big breasts jiggled as I lifted each heavy pumpkin into my sore arms. My nipples had grown ultra-sensitive due to their suckling and now with the sunlight beating down on them, they appeared redder than I'd ever seen them. I hoped I wasn't getting a sunburn there. I did, however, soothe them as I rubbed my hot, tender buds against the outer flesh of the cold pumpkins.

The prison guards never mentioned what had happened earlier and my thoughts continued to churn with ideas of how I could use their sexual interest in me to my benefit.

During my second break in the afternoon, the men instructed me to put on my bra and top. To my disappointment the chains came back on my wrists and I felt defeated.

About two hours later I was instructed to get into their prison van. Then they drove me back to the prison. Before I left the van,

Dixon muttered a see you tomorrow morning, which had excitement pummelling me.

Thankfully, I was put back into solitary confinement instead of general population. Here, in my cell, I spent the rest of my evening napping, doing some reading, playing solitaire on my laptop, eating supper and being alone with my naughty thoughts about how the two prison guards had suckled my nipples so intensely that I'd orgasmed. That had never happened to me before. Climaxing just because my nipples had been so hotly stimulated with their incredibly talented lips was something new and electrifying.

By bedtime I was so aroused at thinking about what Dixon and Ashton had done to me that I was ready for a good round of masturbating.

Lights dimmed at eleven and I waited for a little while. Finally, I heard the guard's footsteps pause in the hallway outside my cell. The little door on the Peeping Tom window slid open so he could look inside. He was doing a head count, making sure I hadn't escaped.

They did that throughout the night and it irritated me that my privacy was invaded on such a routine basis. But hey, I was in prison, so privacy was pretty much non-existent.

When I heard the little door slide back into place, I pushed the blanket off my naked body, lifted my knees and spread my legs wide.

Chapter Five

Then I let me imagination carry me away. My hands smoothed over my nipples and boy, they sure were tender. But I also realized the added tenderness gave my nipples an extra shot of pleasure pain when I touched them.

I imagined Dixon and Ashton's eager mouths at my breasts again. Their lips sensually tugging and sipping. Their tongues lusciously licking and lapping like it happened this morning.

I moaned softly as I gently pinched my nipples and massaged my heaving breasts, gasping as exquisite pleasure quickly sparked to life and whipped through me at my intimate touches.

The desire for an orgasm arrowed along to my lower belly and into my aching vagina. Just as it had this morning.

Eagerness pummeled me as I reached between my thighs and rubbed my fingers around and over my ultrasensitive clitoris. Then I dipped my digits into my vagina for some lube. I smoothed my wet fingers over my clit, tenderly massaging and then dipped into my vagina again.

Anticipation quickly erupted and I fought to remain in control as I stroked around my vagina and tugged at my pussy lips. My juices were spilling from me now and my body was tightening with awareness as I imagined Dixon and Ashton there at my breasts again.

I spread my thighs wider and stroked my palm over my lower belly, caressing my tight flesh and breathing through the erotic shivers of anticipation. Heat flayed my body as I continued to pinch my nipple and thrust two fingers in and out of my vagina. Then I withdrew and rubbed my swollen clitoris before pistoning my fingers into my vagina again, fuelling the inferno of need there.

My body tightened and my breaths grew harsh. Slurping sounds split the air as my fingers thrust faster. The pleasure shudders slammed into me, making me cry out at their intensity.

But I didn't care if the prison guards heard me as the convulsions embraced me like an invisible lover. Explosive pleasure whiplashed through my body, making me writhe like a shaking ragdoll. I twisted and bucked within the beautiful agony, holding onto the shudders for as long as I could until the pleasure disappeared, leaving me panting and perspiring.

Wow, that had been quite intense.

I closed my eyes and just lay there, naked and spent, not caring if a guard came by and checked up on me. Let them look.

Suddenly, I couldn't wait to get back to that pumpkin patch in the morning. To hell with bartering. I knew I would give the prison guards anything they wanted.

They were bastards. They had turned on my sexuality once again and I didn't want it to stop.

I smiled, closed my eyes and slept.

The next morning I was so ready to get back outside the prison walls and happily have some more sex with the two prison guards. To my surprise, I didn't ride back to the pumpkin patch with the other women of the chain gang like I did yesterday morning. Instead, I was instructed to hop into the van with officers Dixon and Ashton.

Both remained silent.

Dixon drove.

He kept peering at me in the rear-view mirror, which made me both uncomfortable and aroused.

Despite their silence, I sensed both men were quite tense with eagerness. Lust shone in their hot gazes and their wide shoulders seemed taut beneath their uniforms.

As we drove into the country, I soaked up the brilliant autumn colors. The bright blue sky, the auburn and crimson laden trees in the distance and the yellowing fields. We drove past a couple of chain gangs consisting of orange suited prison women who were raking the colorful leaves or collecting garbage in the ditches beside the same road I'd travelled yesterday. Soon we turned onto the gravel road and then the same farmer's lane.

The van came to a stop and the two officers jumped out.

My heart was beating a mile a minute as the van's side door slid open. Dixon stood there and he stared at me, saying nothing.

What was he thinking? Could he read my excitement? Or did he think they had gone too far with me yesterday and had decided to stop so they wouldn't get caught?

Oh, I hoped it was not the latter. I held my breath and waited for his next move.

"We have a proposal for you. We'll discuss it at first break. Out of the van. Time to work," he said.

Both frustration and exhilaration whirled through me as I stepped out of the van and into the fresh air and sunshine, my wrist and ankle chains clinking through the quiet air. To my surprise, Dixon removed my wrist restraints.

A moment later I was once again in the pumpkin patch, cutting thick stems and hauling the bright orange pumpkins to the wooden bins while the two ornaments watched and spoke with each other in hushed whispers.

By the time break arrived I was tired and so thirsty I downed the first huge paper cup of water that Ashton produced for me and then I had the nerve to ask for a second helping. Thankfully, I got no protest.

Dixon went to the van and returned with a second cup of delicious ice-cold water.

"Looks hard working out there alone, Mad. How would you feel if we helped you out until lunch?" Dixon asked.

"Suit yourself," I answered as I sat down on the ground.

Perspiration dripped from my forehead, my back ached, and my thighs were getting sore from all that squatting to pick up the heavy pumpkins. I was glad of the offer, but I wasn't getting my hopes up. From my experience prison guards just stood around looking for trouble.

"We know you like to get rewarded ahead of time." Dixon said.

He let his sentence hang in the air for a few seconds, and I was instantly alert.

"What do you propose?" I asked, trying very hard not to appear interested.

Hell, last night, before, during and after masturbating, I'd been ready to do anything they wanted but today after a good night sleep, I was back to thinking about what I would get out of this. It would be really stupid of me to give away free sex when I could get something in return.

"You'll also get an extra half hour for lunch," Ashton added.

"After you get that, you give us what we want," Dixon said in a cool tone.

"What's that?"

"To suck your nipples again for one. And your pussy," he replied.

My breath backed up in my lungs at this new request. My vagina clenched with wicked anticipation as I imagined having the two men going down on me.

I didn't say anything. Didn't want to appear eager, but I could hardly wait for it to happen.

"And to outfit you with a butt plug," Ashton added.

Shock reverberated through me. I continued to remain silent, realizing what was eventually going to happen. Anal sex and possibly a threesome in the near future. An awesome awareness blew through my body and my mind. This was too good to be true.

The two guards stared at me waiting for my answer. I could read the hunger in their eyes. Could feel their need zipping through the air between us. Could feel arousal slamming into me.

Just thinking about them seeing me entirely naked made me feel heady in a really nice way.

"I've got conditions," I hedged.

Dixon frowned. Ashton appeared eager though.

"An offer of assistance and extra lunch time isn't enough for you?" Dixon growled. He appeared angry, but I suspected it was all an act to keep me in line. I decided not to buckle.

"I want a proper lunch. No prison food. And this suckling needs to happen on a nice cozy blanket, like the one I saw in the van. I want a nice warm ass out of the deal."

Dixon chuckled.

"So, you want to be treated like a prison queen, instead of the lowly prisoner that you are."

"I am a queen," I stated firmly. "And if you want this to go any further then you will start to treat me like a queen out here. That means helping with the work all the time. And if you want to knock me up eventually and live out your pregnant woman fancies, then by all means knock me up."

I couldn't believe how bold I had gotten. I noticed the tips of Dixon's lips turn upward ever so slightly. I could tell he was barely keeping it together. I dropped my gaze to the area between his thighs and watched the big erection tent his pants.

Oh yeah, his pregnancy fetish was my hook, and I could tell Dixon was hooked as his eyes got so wide with excitement that I swear I could see the wheels turning inside his brain.

"I'll have to think on the pregnancy. Not sure if we'd be allowed around you if we got you pregnant."

"Then you'll have to make sure they don't find out, won't you?" I answered in a cool voice.

Wow, I really was going too far with this, wasn't I? But I would not allow myself to get pregnant, or would I? Maybe I would just play them for as long as I could. Maybe one day I'd have them wrapped so much around my little finger, they'd help me escape. Wouldn't that be something.

"Okay, we'll meet your conditions. After lunch, you belong to us," Dixon growled. His aqua blue eyes flashed with obvious enjoyment.

"But until then, we want you working topless out there with us. The scenery will get us in a really good mood," Ashton said.

I nodded, trying hard not to tremble from the awakening coursing like liquid fire through my veins. Yesterday I enjoyed having the two men watch my breasts. I also loved having my breasts free with the warm sunshine beating down on my tender nipples. Then I could soothe the achy need of imagining the men suckling at my nipples by rubbing my tender red buds against the cold pumpkins. I would do the same today.

"We have a deal," I replied.

As I unzipped my jumpsuit, I smiled inwardly as the two prison guards watched my every moment.

Chapter Six

Slowly, seductively, I slipped my arms out of the suit like I had done yesterday, and then I removed my top. A moment later, my bra was off and my big breasts spilled free of their restraints.

I could barely wait until after lunch when my lower half was just as free.

To my surprise the two prison guards labored quickly and efficiently. Neither spoke to me nor to each other as they sliced stems and carried the pumpkins to the bins.

When lunchtime rolled around, I was quite ready to skip it and go straight to the sex, but Dixon and Ashton were sticking to the agreement and produced a delicious looking fried chicken breast, some potato salad, a huge slice of French style bread and a sealed container of green salad along with some packets of French dressing. Plus a thermos of delicious black coffee.

Man, I was drooling just looking at this food. It surely was a feast fit for a queen and it was all displayed on that snug looking blanket I had requested from the back of the van.

I devoured the food, eating topless, ignoring the two prison guards as they watched me from afar. They ate quietly, and I knew they had given me a share of their lunch. But I didn't care.

The prison lunch would have been the same as always. A boring sandwich, along with bottled water and some tinned dessert of fruit or pudding, depending on the day. This food and the coffee, made love to my taste buds and after I was finished eating I simply lay down upon the blanket, satiated. I stared up at the bright blue sky, feeling better than I had in years.

Heaven. I felt like I was in Heaven, having had such a delicious meal. It was the first decent meal since I had been shipped off to prison.

I felt sleepy and closed my eyes. It would be just for a few minutes as I was sure I had not used the entire lunch hour. The two men would come when it was their time with me.

I languished in the warmth of the bright autumn sunlight and felt all my aches and pains disintegrate as I drifted off, wrapped in memories of the red-hot sex I'd had with my ex, the man I had accidentally killed. Yeah, he'd been an asshole but he'd been unquenchable in bed. He'd given me plenty of orgasms as long as I reciprocated, and I'd been eager to please.

I wouldn't be so eager to please these two prison guards. I had learned my lesson not to give too much unless I got something in return first. People would have to earn my trust. Not that I could ever trust these two. Especially in the situation I now found myself in.

A strange noise filtered through my drowsiness and I slowly opened my eyes.

Dixon and Ashton stood on each side of me. They were staring down at me with their predatory gazes and my breath halted as I realized both men were completely nude. They possessed big erections. Long and thick cocks.

"Your time is up. Our time has begun," Dixon said in a guttural voice. He was ready to get on with this and so was I, but why were they naked? I hadn't agreed to them actually penetrating me. At least not yet.

I blinked as Dixon held out his hand.

"You need to stand so you can get out of your clothes," he said.

His blue eyes were on fire and I felt the heat moving through me as well.

I noticed he was holding out a key.

"Remove your shoes and socks first and then the ankle restraints. Don't even think about running or tossing away the key. We have an emergency one," Dixon growled.

And here I thought he was holding out his hand because he was going to help me to my feet. Chivalry was indeed dead.

I did as he instructed and removed my shoes and socks while they watched. Then I grabbed the key from him and jammed it into the lock, loving the sound of the click. In a moment, I removed the ankle cuffs and let the chains rattle as I tossed them aside into the tall grass.

I placed the key into one shoe.

A moment later, I stood, trying to ignore the fact that I was actually free of all restraints. I would have made a run for it, but yeah, no shoes. I'd freeze my feet off in the cold dirt. Besides, I was eager to have Dixon and Ashton's mouths upon my flesh and they were putting on a good show, stroking their erections.

They watched as I stepped out of my jumper. Beneath the jumper I wore prison issue track pants and panties. I slid my fingers beneath the waistband of the clothing and slowly, seductively lowered my pants and panties over my hips and then down my legs. I removed my garments and faced the two men.

Their eyes blazed fire as they visually caressed my naked curves. Their erections had thickened and were flushed red with arousal. My pussy grew hot and swollen and I was creaming hot juices, reacting to the stimulating sight.

"Lie down on the blanket, Queen," Dixon instructed.

My heart cracked like a jackhammer as I lay upon the blanket. The wonderful sunshine beat down on my naked body, embracing me with its intense heat.

"No touching us under any circumstances. If you do, the restraints will be placed on you for the rest of the workday. Understood?" Dixon growled.

I nodded and wondered what the big deal was with them not wanting me to touch them. Were they afraid I was going to wrap an arm around their neck and break it? Or maybe they thought I was going to strangle their balls? I grinned inwardly at those thoughts.

"Lift your knees. Spread your legs," Ashton ordered.

His voice sounded hoarse, and the lust flaring in his brown eyes made me tremble. He ripped open a package and pulled out a pink butt plug. It was pretty big and I wondered if it would hurt.

"Have you worn one of these before?" Ashton asked as he held it up.

"Yes, years ago," I admitted.

"Good. This plug comes already sterile and ready to use. I'll put on lots of lube so it will be go in easy enough. I will insert it. Wear it up to a couple of hours at a time. Start slow. You'll get a tube of lube smuggled in with your supper tonight. I'll put these instructions into your pocket. If anyone finds it, say you found it in the orchard. You won't be lying."

A tube of lube with my supper? Wow, he had that good connections?

He reached down and shoved the instructions into my jumper pocket.

"When we think you're ready for anal, we'll make more concessions where work is concerned. Agreed?"

"Yes," I whispered. Heat fused my cheeks and I was eager to continue.

"I'll put the plug in, after..." he said softly.

My breaths were coming faster at his words. I now realized there seriously would be anal penetration sometime down the line and more work concessions. It appeared sex with my prison guards was going to be an ongoing thing, which really thrilled me. Life in prison just got exciting!

Dixon sat down, cross legged on my left side. He slid his hand between his muscular legs and wrapped his fingers around his thick cock. I gasped as his shaft jerked in his hand.

Such fierce power in that gorgeous looking vein riddled rod. I wanted him thrusting into me, but sensed it wasn't going to happen today. The bastards were teasing me in exposing to me their shafts. Showing me what could be mine. Preparing me for what was coming down the line.

The visual stimulation of seeing Dixon cradling his penis, shot wicked want into me. I was so close to telling them that I wanted them to fuck me with their cocks but I held back. I couldn't give into my full needs, not until I had more concessions from them and I needed their trust in me too so I could use them to make my life easier on the inside.

I clenched my hands into the blankets, resisting the urge to touch Dixon's muscular chest. I didn't want to be in restraints for the rest of the day.

I held my breath as Dixon reached out and cupped my breast with his other hand. He held me like he owned me and licked his lips like he was about to devour something magnificent.

A powerful gush of eagerness raged through me as he lowered his head over my breast.

I moaned as Dixon sucked my tender nipple between his hot firm lips. My plump, red nipple was even more sensitive than yesterday due to what they'd done to me, so there was a tiny bite of pain which actually enhanced the pleasure his mouth was creating.

He must have sensed my discomfort, for he sipped leisurely, like I was a precious wine, not forcefully as yesterday.

Then Ashton's shoulders, pushed against my feet as he lowered himself between my spread knees. He was licking his red lips as he stared at my pussy and a wicked need zipped through me as I awaited his next move.

I didn't have to wait long.

He kissed my inner thighs. His hot mouth caressing my flesh, moving slowly until my thighs were trembling and my body was humming. Then hot hands replaced his mouth and he smoothed his palms up and down, igniting shards of heat.

I gasped at the intensity of his ministrations and found myself creaming easily. I moaned as his palms turned into fingers and he softly stroked toward the clenching apex of my thighs. I hadn't been touched by a man down there for over five years and my pussy was aching for male attention.

I cried out as his fingers touched my labia. Moaned as he pulled apart my pussy lips and dipped two fingers into my wet vagina.

Chapter Seven

My body tightened with expectation as he withdrew and then his sopping fingers slid over my tender clitoris in mind-destroying strokes. He took my tender clit between thumb and fore finger and began a gentle rub that had me writhing and crying out as ravaging pleasure suddenly exploded throughout me.

I was a bomb that had been detonated as he cuddled my clit. I twisted within the pleasure that snapped through me in quivering waves. His voracious mouth fused over my pussy and I screamed as his long, hot tongue slid into my vagina like a little cock, prodding and thrusting against my spasming muscles.

Shuddering convulsions destroyed me and I quickly became a bucking tornado as Ashton eagerly sucked my cream into his mouth.

I felt as if I was now just a hot swollen pussy and one turgid nipple as the men lapped, licked, and stroked.

Raging pleasure sunk bone deep, ripping apart my thoughts and every shred of self-control. I was their puppet, and they were my masters as their mouths slammed pleasure into me over and over until my brain was fried and I was screaming within the climaxes that were easily wrung from me.

Deep down in the back of what was left of my mind, I sensed that Ashton had a pussy juice fetish and he would suck and pleasure me for as long as it took for me to keep producing my cream.

Sweet mercy! My two prison guards had turned me into a vessel for their fetishes and now I was lost within the pleasure they created. I knew I would keep bucking and writhing until they deemed this session was over.

Perspiration blossomed over my flesh as they kept sucking on me. No more thoughts were processing. I was just gone, replaced by an insane machine of lust that would just keep producing for them.

Dear heavens, would I go mad from this exquisite torture?

By the time Officers Dixon and Ashton were finished sucking on me, I was panting and keening from the exquisite pleasure. I'd heard both of them come on groans and strangled gasps while they'd mouth pleasured me. They must have been masturbating while my eyes had been closed and I'd been nicely trapped inside their pleasure vortex.

I was spent after their mouths finally left me. I thought it was over, but then I heard the slurp of lube and remembered the butt plug.

"On your hands and knees, Queen. We need to get you outfitted, then we need to get back to work. We need to meet a certain quota," Ashton ordered.

I kind of liked how they'd nicknamed me Queen. There didn't appear to be sarcasm in Ashton's voice as he'd said it, so I hoped they'd gotten the message when I'd told them I was a queen and wanted to be treated better.

I could barely move but I managed to turn over and got onto my fours upon the rumpled blanket. My vagina was raw and open after being sucked so much and my inner thighs were sticky from my cream. My big breasts hung down and I noticed how red and extra plump my one nipple had gotten from Dixon's eager mouth. It felt bruised and used, but nicely so.

"You'll enjoy wearing this plug, I'm sure. Once your ass has becomes accustomed to it, there are bigger sizes," Ashton said from behind me.

"Yes, we want our Queen to be open and juicy for us," Dixon said as he slipped on his underwear. I almost moaned as I watched his limp shaft disappear inside the garment. He was smiling happily as he slipped on his prison issue uniform and was gone.

It appeared he had gotten the satisfaction he'd wanted by sucking my cream out of me.

I hissed as Ashton's lubed finger suddenly pressed against my sphincter. He wasn't wasting any time, was he?

"Just stay loose and relax," he muttered.

Easier said than done when someone was trying to stick a finger into my back door. But I did the best I could and impulsively moaned some more when my tight ring of muscles gave way and he slipped his digit inside.

"I should take you right now. Your pussy cream was so delicious that I came just from the taste of it," he whispered.

"Do you think I'm your slut?" I hissed back at him. I wanted him to take me but I was exhausted, mentally and physically.

I also wanted to remind him I should be treated like a Queen, or at least as best as a prisoner who is giving free sex to her guards should be treated.

"You're not our slut, you are our saviour," he growled.

I stiffened at his confession.

"How so?" I asked.

He said nothing as he withdrew his finger. The slurp of lube followed. I moaned as he pressed two slippery fingers inside my anus.

"You're saving our marriages. Our wives won't cater to our fetishes, so we come to the prison girls, like you."

So, they were married. Disappointment rocked me. They were going behind their wives back. That meant they were not to be trusted. Ever.

"Glad I can be of assistance," I muttered.

He remained silent after that. Perhaps he realized he'd said too much? I gasped as my muscles clenched like a vice around his fingers.

He withdrew. More slurps of lube followed and then something larger than his two fingers pushed against my sphincter. I knew it was the smooth narrow head of the butt plug. I could feel that it had been generously lubed too.

"Just relax," he once again instructed.

I blew out a tense breath and he slowly, cautiously pushed in. It got bigger because of the flared area and then it got narrow again until it was in.

I felt relieved and concentrated on the foreign object buried inside of me. It was an invasion, but I knew from past experience I would get used to it fast.

"Now, we need to get back to work," Ashton instructed. He said nothing more as he hurriedly dressed and then he headed out to the field. To my surprise, Dixon was out there, cutting the stems on the pumpkins.

Huh, now look at that. The ornaments were actually working again. Who would have figured?

I reached for my clothes, feeling the butt plug stretching into my ass with my every movement. Suddenly I wished one of the men was taking me back there. To feel a cock thrusting in and out of my ass would be nice. I remember my asshole ex had enjoyed anal to the point where I'd found myself enjoying it as well.

Heck, I'd take anal over picking pumpkins.

I chuckled to myself and didn't move extra fast in dressing myself. After I had my clothing on, I slipped on my socks and shoes and then I froze.

They'd forgotten to shackle me.

I could run for it.

Good heavens! I should make a run for it!!

I'd just had the most fantastic sex with the two prison guards and now an opportunity to escape had come my way. It should be a no brainer. Run or not to run? The question danced in my head as I watched Dixon and Ashton working in the field. They didn't so much as look my way.

I stood and kept studying them.

Had they left the restraints off on purpose? Were they testing me? If so, and I decided to run, they would surely catch me, especially now with me being exhausted after feeding them with my body. If I took off they would drop me as their sexual host and pick some other prison girl for their pleasures and I wanted to be pleasured by them. At least for now.

Another idea began to form.

I closed my eyes and cursed myself for what I was about to do.

I headed back to the field and joined them. Was I an idiot? Or was I smart for not running?

Dixon and Ashton looked up as I approached but said nothing and quickly returned to the pumpkin work. I pretended not to notice I was restraint free. It was best if they thought I was a docile submissive...well kind of.

Hopefully, this wasn't a one-time occurrence in them forgetting, that is if they forgot. If they had, then yeah, I was an idiot for not taking the opportunity. But if they began to see I wasn't going to run, then I could get their trust and maybe, just maybe, they would leave the restraints off and I would have a better shot at an escape in the future, especially if I could figure out how to get a hold of that prison van.

It was a chance I was willing to take in staying, especially for more of that naughty sex I'd just had.

We worked quietly. We took our breaks separately and at the end of the workday, Dixon produced the restraints and within a minute I was once again in them. But I didn't feel dejected anymore. I had hope now. And some more hot sex on the horizon. No complaints here. Except for the prison food.

As promised a tube of lube was stashed beneath a napkin when my tray with supper was delivered through the slot. I didn't even bother to gaze up at the guard or wave a hello, which I often did when he slid open the Peeping Tom peep hole to check if I had escaped.

In solitary any face was welcome. But tonight, I was just thinking about tomorrow and the sex.

I found myself wondering if I was experiencing the Stockholm Syndrome phenomenon where a captive begins to have feelings for their captor. I didn't know for sure if I were a case, but I did know I would never develop feelings for them.

I would from here on out use them. I would make them comfortable in trusting me. I would study them. Discover their routine where I was concerned and pay particular attention to the vehicles they used, because a vehicle would be essential in my getaway.

And tonight I wouldn't be doing any masturbating. I'd keep myself excited for them. It would make the sexual contact that much more intense tomorrow.

Chapter Eight

I spent the evening as all the other ones, reading, playing Solitaire on my laptop, supper, and so on, but with one change.

In my mind I'd keep a notebook of all possibilities of escape and when the time came and I had a sure-fire chance of getting out of the prison system and fleeing. I would take it.

I mean I had done half my time here already, but anything could happen to keep me here for years beyond my minimum sentence. It wasn't a chance I was willing to take.

In the meantime, I'd enjoy the sexual perks Dixon and Ashton were handing over to me, which made me wonder what they had in store for me tomorrow.

I smiled.

Tomorrow couldn't get here soon enough.

THE NEXT MORNING WAS my access to the shower. We were able to shower three times a week in the shower room. That's another reason I enjoyed solitary. I showered alone, except for the female guard on the other side of the open stall.

After my shower I dressed, had breakfast and was ready to head out.

Promptly I was picked up by one of the guards in charge at solitary. I was escorted to where Dixon and Ashton waited in the garage at the prison van. I noted it was the same vehicle as yesterday. Same licence plate.

I was ushered inside the van, with wrist and leg restraints, and while we drove, the two men remained silent as always.

Ashton drove and I could see he was glancing at me in the rear-view mirror every once in awhile. I don't know why as there was a camera in an upper corner behind him. Unless it wasn't working.

I ignored him and began to take inventory of the interior of the van.

The screened partition between the two guards and me was padlocked and it would prevent me from jumping them. Not that I could overpower two men.

The two exits all had screen doors too and I assumed padlocked on the other side.

There was nothing in here except the uncomfortable metal seats and the windows that allowed me to see that today was a cloudy day outside. It looked dreary and grey. A lot of the colorful leaves had left their trees, leaving most of them barren.

In conclusion of my inspection I could see there was nothing in here that I could use as a weapon in a future escape attempt. But that didn't dismay me. I'd just keep my eyes open for opportunities. Surely there would be better ones than the one I'd had yesterday.

We drove along the same long lone highway as always. Finally I spotted a couple of prison vans that were parked in secluded laneways as we passed. Then came a couple of chain gangs of eight women in each gang who were raking leaves and picking up garbage out of the ditches. I recognized a couple of the women whom I'd travelled with in a prison van on my first day out of the prison.

To think I had narrowly missed being there in the ditch with them. I was quite thrilled I was having sex instead of listening to bitchy cronies and raking all day or picking up garbage.

Moments later we turned onto the same gravel road we'd previously used, but this time we stopped earlier, which made me pray that there were no pumpkins on the other side of this row of evergreen trees.

I'd grown sick of picking pumpkins. My arms, thighs and back were sore from all that bending and lifting. But I wasn't sick of the sex. I needed to be pleasured today, especially because I hadn't taken the edge off last night.

"Alright, Queen. Time to work," Dixon said as he slid open the side door and that's when I realized there was no padlock on that metal barred screen as he slid it open. Why had I never noticed that before?

Excitement rushed through me as I jumped out of the van.

Had the padlock always been missing?

Man, becoming observant certainly did raise opportunities of escape.

"Still wearing your plug?" Ashton asked as he and Dixon ushered me through the row of dense pine trees.

"Yes, as you instructed. I'm taking care of it. No worries," I replied brightly. I wanted him to think I was being submissive.

Inside I chuckled. But my chuckling stalled when I spied what we'd be doing today.

"Apple trees?" I questioned as I stared along the rows and rows of trees heavily laden with bright red apples. My mouth watered as I imagined biting into one.

"You'll be picking and we'll be dumping and sorting," Dixon answered.

"Can we eat them?" I asked, suddenly realizing I had fresh fruit.

"As many as you want, " he said.

Wow! Cool! This was good. I loved apples and it was rare to get a nice red one in prison. Having them fresh off a tree was something I'd never experienced before.

Dixon proceeded to hand me a lightweight yellow plastic basket with a handle. There was a hook dangling off the handle.

"Hang the basket by hooking the hook on the nearby branches as you pick. You'll start picking around the bottom of the trees. Handle the apples like eggs. Then you grab a ladder and start your way up.

Bring the full baskets to us at the bin." He pointed to several aluminum twenty-foot ladders that had been leaned against a nearby tree and then to the row of wood slat bins that were laid out down the rows of apple trees.

"Hold out your hands," Dixon said in a cool command. His blue eyes seemed icy cold in the grey ambiance of our surroundings.

I did as I was told, feeling excitement shift through me as he uncuffed my wrists and then he let the chains drop into the grass.

"Undo her leg restraints," he ordered Ashton, who stood nearby.

The cool autumn wind was blowing from behind Ashton and I caught a gentle whiff of soap. He smelled good. I liked a clean man who smelled good, especially when I was going to have sex with him.

Ashton nodded and did as he was told. I would have had a clear shot at the back of his neck if I'd had a weapon, but I noticed Dixon had placed his hand on the handle of his gun.

Okay, he didn't trust me. Yet.

"And what did you want in return today for allowing me to go without restraints?" I asked.

"You'll be wearing an ankle monitor instead of restraints. You'll be able to climb the ladder easier."

My hopes plummeted at the mention of the ankle monitor.

Damn! I should have known. No escape today.

"We'll discuss a proposition for you at first break," Ashton said as he quickly put on the ankle monitor.

And just like that, my hopes were high again.

No escape today, but definitely some red-hot sex!

I could hardly wait for break-time to find out what they had in store for me!

The job went easy enough and when break time came, I was eager to find out what the two prison guards would propose they wanted to do sexually to me. If I played my cards right, in return for my submission, they'd be doing my job hauling the heavy baskets of apples to the bin and I would be doing their job of dumping and sorting.

At break, I received my traditional tall paper cup filled with ice-cold water and then a second helping. They'd also supplied a nice, folded blanket for me to sit on while I stared off into the distance at the tall yellowing grass beneath the apple-laden trees we still had to work on. I figured we'd be here for at least a few more days. The area was secluded, just like the pumpkin patch had been.

I'd munched on several apples while working in the trees or up the ladder. The fruit was juicy and so delicious and sweet that I wondered how I could smuggle a couple of apples back into the prison with me. I doubted I could get one inside because every time I returned from being outdoors, I was physically patted down and a metal detector waved all around my body parts.

I was crunching on yet another sweet apple as I sat waiting for them to make their proposition for today.

Finally, they approached and towered over me while I continued to sit. The air was getting warmer now, and thankfully the sun was peeking out from between the clouds splashing sunshine here and there.

"We have a proposition for you, for after lunch," Dixon said. His eyes weren't as icy cold now that the weather was improving which for some crazy reason made me feel better.

"Okay, shoot," I said after swallowing a bite.

"Yesterday you had the pleasure of oral from me," Ashton said. "I'd like you to return the favor on me."

I inhaled at that idea. I'd done oral to my late ex many times so I knew what to do.

I turned to look up at Dixon.

"And you?"

"I'll be taking him anally while you do him orally."

Oh. Okay. This was different. However there was just one problem.

"What pleasures do I get out of the deal?" I requested directly.

"What did you want?" Dixon asked.

Wow, a wide-open possibility. The thought about forgoing being pleasured today and simply getting them to work for me the rest of the day shot through my mind. However, I knew I'd be bored with that request. I wanted more.

"Do you have condoms?" I asked.

I noticed both men stiffen.

Chapter Nine

"We do," Ashton replied coolly. He reached into his breast pocket and produced several packets of condoms. He fanned them on the blanket beside me.

"Then I want some red-hot vaginal sex and I want to be able to touch you with one of you taking me while both of you are kissing me. I want to be pleasured like the Queen that I am."

Ashton and Dixon looked at each other with what I could only interpret as an endearing look. Understanding suddenly whipped through me. These two men must be gay or more likely bisexual. Maybe in love with each other? Yesterday Ashton had said I was their savior. That their wives didn't want to do things with them and that was why they came to the prisoners.

"All this is going to cut into the work time," Dixon suddenly said.

Well, if he thought I was going to give up breaks and lunch, he could forget it. However he was neatly falling into my plan.

"Then I suggest you two do the picking and dumping of the apples into the bins and I do the sorting. Two men work much faster than one woman. Deal?"

I held my breath as I awaited their answer.

"Deal," Ashton said. "But after lunch, we go first and then you get pleasured."

Hmm I preferred to have my payment up front, however I realized I was getting a good deal with them doing my job anyways, so why push my luck.

"Deal."

"We start after lunch. Break time is up. Ashton and I will start with the picking now, then we won't have to rush this afternoon," Dixon said. He nodded to his partner and they both headed back to the orchard.

I couldn't stop myself from smiling.

Man, life was getting so much better having these two men around. I would have an easy day of work, do some oral and then get pleasured. Why would I want to escape from that?

I hid my smiles as I headed back to work.

Lunch came quickly and to my surprise, Dixon shared his home-made meal with me. He didn't say anything as he handed me a droolworthy half a foot long submarine sandwich drenched with bacon, tomato, mayo, pickles and lettuce. Ashton gave me a bag of potato chips along with a soft drink can. In prison, we weren't allowed cans for fear we'd use them as missiles when throwing them at someone or makeshift shanks made out of the metal to slice or stab someone.

So, having a can in my hand, was bliss. It also meant trust was forming with them towards me. And that in my book was a good thing.

They strolled down a ways and ate by themselves, speaking in hushed tones like lovers would do. The way they smiled at each other made me think that yeah, something was going on between them. But it wasn't my business. I just wanted some pleasure and an easy workday.

Eagerness barrelled through me, as a little while later, Dixon gazed at his watch. He said something to Ashton, who looked my way and then he nodded.

I'd finished lunch a long time ago and had been trying hard not to let what was about to happen get in the way of me relaxing in the sunshine. But it did get in the way and I couldn't wait to touch them because I hadn't touched a man in so long that it was insane.

I gazed down at the condoms that had been placed on the blankets and shivered as my pussy clenched with an intense need for penetration. I would be getting some good old-fashioned sex after I gave the men what they wanted.

I held my breath as I saw the two prison guards approaching.

Show time.

Ashton and Dixon removed their weapon laden utility belts and placed them upon some nearby bushes. Then they detached their radios and took off their shoes. Their uniforms came next as I watched them.

I was feeling pretty flushed as their muscle-toned bodies emerged. They were in really good shape. I had noticed it yesterday but too many naughty things were happening to me for me to fully comprehend and appreciate these men's bodies.

Just thinking about what they wanted me to do to Ashton had me energized. The two prison guards had fetishes, yet they were also gay, but more likely bisexual as they'd gotten aroused seeing me naked.

Maybe they were closet bisexuals? Whatever they were, I needed to remind myself that their sexual orientation really was none of my business.

They looked dominant and dangerous, their eyes full of lust as they gazed at each other and continued to undress. Power oozed off their hard bodies in heated waves. They were two men on a mission as their cocks unfurled from the restraints of their underwear. They were both fully erect. Aroused and engorged. They were exceptionally well hung and their long thick shafts were ready for action.

My heart began to pound as they dropped their garments onto a heap beside the blanket.

"Get undressed," Dixon growled at me. "We want you naked."

I nodded meekly and did their bidding, placing my clothing beside theirs, keeping note of how easy it would be right at this moment for me to slip a gun out of one of their holsters and point it at them. Maybe shoot them dead and make a getaway.

But I wasn't ready yet. I needed more details. Like did they check in with the prison during the day? What times? Where did they keep the keys to the prison van? How would I be able to escape without being noticed when I was in that van? Where would I go when I made a run for it?

Too many things to think about and a bunch of problems to solve. When I made my escape, I wanted it to go smoothly. There would be more opportunities soon. I would have to wait until I had a vivid plan, preparing for all contingencies.

I had a butt plug up my ass. That was my insurance that they would be keeping me around for a little while anyways. In the meantime, I could get more enjoyment out of these two.

My breaths came faster and I swallowed, then I nervously licked my lips, preparing myself for Ashton. I hadn't done oral on a man in years, but it was kind of like riding a bicycle, you never forgot how to do it.

Ashton came and stood in front of me.

"On your knees, and sit up straight, Queen," he ordered.

I did as instructed and got on my knees, sitting straight so that my breasts poked out at him.

"Don't try anything funny. No strangling my balls or biting my cock off or you'll disappear without a trace. Is that clear?" Ashton said.

His voice was cold and I knew he was serious. I suddenly realized I had to be very careful with his sensitive part. I also grasped that there was a good chance that they would do away with me anyways once they fulfilled their future fantasies. I would be a loose end if I decided to talk and they would be in deep shit if someone in the prison system believed me.

Dread dropped over me like a cold blanket and my innocence was gone. I got the creepy feeling my days might be numbered. That plan I was devising would have to come sooner rather than later if I were to survive these two prison guards.

I nodded and forced myself not to think about what might happen in the future. Right now I was safe and I would enjoy myself.

Man, maybe I was a Stockholm Syndrome case after all?

"You know what to do," Ashton said as he gazed down at me.

I reached out and gingerly curled one hand around the base of his thick shaft. His flesh felt hot and it jerked as I started stroking up and down his length. His penis grew even bigger and bigger and he began moaning.

His gaze was intense as he reached out. His long fingers slid through my hair at the sides of my head. He gripped me hard, holding my head steady and then he moved his hips forward.

His cockhead was a mere inch from my face and I opened my mouth, suddenly eager to please. Hell, I'd better please or I *would* mysteriously disappear.

Behind him, I heard Dixon ripping open a condom package. Moments later, the heavy slurps of lube followed. My vaginal muscles clenched at the erotic sounds. Soon it would be my turn, but first Ashton needed his pleasure.

Pulsing hot lust shot through me as he pushed his feverish cockhead into my mouth.

Ashton's shaft stretched and burned my quaking lips and I wasted no time in moving my head forward, allowing him to slide in further. I stopped when he touched the back of my throat.

Then I moved my head back about an inch and wrapped my other hand around his cock right outside my mouth so when he withdrew and began to thrust, my hand would prevent his penis from going all the way into my throat and making me gag.

I gave him a nod and Ashton began a slow drive, in and out, and I tightened my lips around his penis, giving him a good pressure. Suddenly there came a bit of a buck and Ashton's cock slid deeper and I heard him gasp.

That meant Dixon had to be penetrating him anally now. I looked up at Ashton's face and saw his mouth hanging open and his eyes scrunched tight. His pistoning became faster and I hollowed out my cheeks giving him more compression.

He moaned and gasped again. He liked what Dixon and I were doing to him.

Ashton's cock filled my mouth and then he withdrew. Then Dixon penetrated him again, pushing Ashton's shaft back into my mouth. Over and over we went. We got into an arousing rhythm and before long both men were moaning and groaning.

Whimpers escaped my mouth as I grew excited and needy imagining both of these prison guards eventually thrusting into me. My nipples elongated, my ass clenched around the plug and my pussy juices began to seep out of me.

My mouth was seared with heat and my lips felt bruised as Ashton continued plunging in and out. His cock thickened and jerked in my mouth and his breaths grew faster and faster. His thrusts grew harder and harder.

Chapter Ten

"I'm coming!" Ashton suddenly cried out.

A few more solid thrusts and then hot jets of his release flooded my mouth. Quickly I swallowed and kept sucking and sucking on his hot spasming flesh until he was dry.

Then he removed his cock from my mouth and Dixon withdrew from Ashton, who then wearily sat down at the edge of the blanket beside me. His breathing was harsh and his eyes were dark with excitement.

"That was so good," Ashton complimented.

"Glad to be of service," Dixon replied, his eyes twinkling with happiness as he carefully removed the condom from his very erect cock. I could tell that Dixon liked that Ashton had experienced a good release.

"Take her," he breathed, nodding to Dixon's big erection.

Dixon grinned and leaned over his clothing to pick up a small packet of wet wipes. Quickly he cleaned his hands with one and tossed the package to me.

Goodness, these men came prepared. I wiped my hands and whimpered as Dixon grabbed a new condom and quickly sheathed it onto his engorged penis.

His blue eyes glimmered like jewels as he held out his hand to me.

"Stand, Queen," he ordered in a guttural tone.

Huh, I guess chivalry wasn't dead after all.

I placed my palm against his and he easily hoisted me to my feet. Then he let go and his hands slid upon my hips like two scorching brands of possession.

"You can touch me as per our agreement. Ashton will do the same to you," Dixon whispered in a rasping tone.

Ashton was back on his feet and had stepped behind me. His body heat whipped against my back, warming me and I shuddered as his hot hands cupped my ass cheeks. He leaned against me and began fanning feather light kisses across the back of my shoulders. It felt so good to finally be touched by a man again and I moaned my thanks.

Dixon's warm breath caressed my face and I trembled as he closed his eyes and lowered his head. His hot mouth slammed over mine in a fierce ownership that had my head spinning. His tongue forced itself between my lips and stroked my teeth and gums, making me heady.

I grabbed his waist, relishing the tautness of his body and held on for dear life as my world tilted. I'd never been kissed so forcefully before, and I felt like a virgin in unfamiliar territory. Sparkles of pleasure snapped through my nipples as he buffed his hot muscular chest all over my breasts.

He squished his cockhead against my engorged clitoris and began rubbing and grinding me there. My lower body tightened, my inner thighs quivered and my pussy felt hot, swollen and dripped with my juices.

I sensed I could come at any minute.

Dixon nipped and suckled at my lips with his kisses, leaving dainty little stings behind as he continued all the way around my mouth. By the time he was finished my upper and lower lips were on fire.

Then his mouth melted over mine again and I felt possessed. He slid his cockhead off my quivering clit and plunged an inch into my wet vagina. His silk-encased flesh throbbed teasingly there.

"Touch me," he whispered as he broke the kiss.

I barely heard him through the buzzing in my ears and the panting of my breath.

I smoothed my hands between our bodies, fanning my palms over his hot chest muscles, feeling them jerk beneath my fingers. I found a nipple and pinched it gently, then rubbed and caressed it until it became rock hard and he was moaning. I did the same to his other nipple until his breaths came hard and fast.

Ashton's hands were smoothing seductively up and down my arms and he was pressing himself against my butt plug. Insistently, but not too hard. The plug felt like a cock buried deep inside my ass. The pressure was intense and bruisingly beautiful.

Was this how it was going to feel when they both finally took me?

I couldn't wait to find out how a threesome with double penetration would unfold, but right now Dixon and Ashton were doing a magnificent job in pleasuring me.

Ashton's kisses intensified. His hot lips danced over the back of my neck making me shiver. The intoxicating way he pushed against my behind making that butt plug move inside my ass had me moaning.

Dixon's mouth was fused over mine, sliding back and forth as his cock worked deeper and deeper into my sopping vagina with every penetration. He was going agonizingly slow because of the tightness created by the plug and I was at the edge of having an orgasm.

I just needed a little extra stimulation.

As if finally sensing what I craved, Dixon withdrew and forcefully drove his cock into me all the way. I shuddered as every thick inch of his solid penis stretched into my ultra-tight vagina.

He pulled out and began a driving thrust. The added friction was exactly what I needed. Spasms exploded throughout and I went wild as an orgasm rocked through me. Shudders embraced me and I bucked and gyrated between the two men.

Dixon was pumping so wickedly and Ashton was moving that butt plug so nicely that I got lost inside the brutal firestorm raging in me.

It was agony, bliss and pleasure, all rolled into one. I was gasping, moaning and keening as my vaginal muscles tightened and quivered and pulsed around Dixon's intrusion and my ass clenched the plug.

Dixon pistoned faster and faster and then he ripped his mouth from mine. He cried out his pleasure as he came.

Somewhere in the back of my mind I knew it the instant it happened. The second his hot release flooded my insides; I knew the condom had broken.

Oh shit.

But I was so wrapped inside my own climax I just couldn't stop my vagina from milking his seed. Couldn't stop gyrating or keening or stopping myself as I flew into a red-hot second orgasm. It rocked me harder than the first one, and both men carried me through it. Their kisses, their heated touches swept over my quivering hot flesh. They knew where to caress me, knew how to keep my pussy milking Dixon for so long that I would have gone on forever, it was so beautiful.

The rush of convulsions was spectacular. Like nothing I had ever experienced before.

Pleasure ravaged me as I mindlessly convulsed between the bodies of the two prison guards. Finally the climax ebbed away and I was physically spent.

Dixon withdrew and surely enough his condom had ripped. He bit his bottom lip, a sheepish smile on his face as he held up the condom for us to see.

"Looks like your pregnancy woman fetish might be coming true after all," Ashton said and elbowed Dixon, who winked at me.

Son of a bitch.

If I didn't know any better, I would think he'd sabotaged that condom in the first place.

My heart was pounding at an insane pace as I plopped down onto the blanket, feeling both dejected and elated, if that was possible.

I could be pregnant. If I were, there really wasn't anything I could do about it anyway, so why fret?

Dixon and Ashton sat down on the blanket with me, then the two men lay down on their sides, facing each other. Dixon ordered me to spoon against his backside, which I obediently did.

A few minutes later, both prison guards were snoring softly.

But I remained wide awake. What if I was pregnant? If I stayed in the prison system Dixon and Ashton might decide to keep me around just because of Dixon's pregnancy fetish. Or they might want to get rid of me because the DNA in the baby would prove we'd had sex.

I had a big decision to make, didn't I? Especially now that I could be thinking for two instead of just me.

To escape and live on the run with a baby or stay in the prison on work detail and take my chances that Dixon and Ashton wouldn't make me disappear.

Things just got seriously complicated.

I had a lot to think about.

The rest of the day went by uneventfully as we worked beneath the gorgeous autumn sunshine.

I'd been watching the guards as they worked and it appeared as if they were not in any regular communication with the prison. They wore their weapons at all times, except for when we had sex. I'd also discovered where they kept the keys to the van.

Whomever drove, put the key into their breast pocket along with the keys to my chains, which I continued to wear before the work began and at the end of the day after we were finished working and before I was ushered back to the van.

A plan of escape was formulating now as the workday drew to a close. A few more days of this routine and more observations, I sensed I might be ready to make my escape attempt.

Back at the prison, in isolation, I opted not to masturbate after lights out, realizing I got more sexual satisfaction from the prison guards.

Pondering that Dixon might have made me pregnant had me seesawing between giddiness and disappointment. Having a baby in prison would be a no no for me. They wouldn't let me keep it, and who would take it? There was no way I would give a kid of mine up for adoption, nor would I abort. The only person I could think of who might stand by me and take my baby was my sister who I hadn't heard from since I'd come in here.

Heck, I didn't even know where she lived.

Having a baby on the run, if I did manage to escape, would be the better option.

The next few days went the same way as the last few. There was no mention of the possibility of my being pregnant but the sex continued to be scorching hot. Ashton inserted a larger butt plug one afternoon and that night a new tube of lube had been delivered with my supper tray just like the last time.

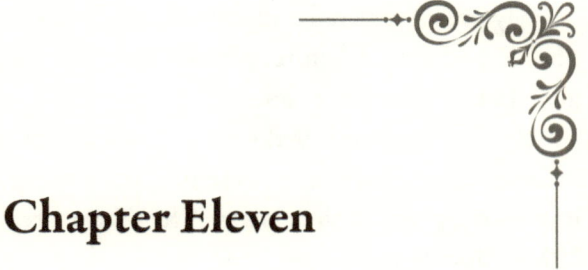

Chapter Eleven

Every new day we agreed on what would happen during sex. I got work concessions and I really did feel like a Queen. The prison guards brought me home-made lunches and I loved all the food. Drench worthy roast beef sandwiches, mouth-watering salmon sandwiches, fresh garden salads, and even cold steak burgers.

My guards were growing careless during and after sex, to the point we were all beginning to take naps after our sessions, spooned against each other on a blanket they always supplied.

Yup, this was as good as freedom. Almost.

Another thing I noticed. I was becoming addicted to sex with my prison guards. I couldn't wait to get to work. Couldn't wait to have sex and at times my plans for freedom would wane.

However, I kept reminding myself that they could and probably would make me mysteriously disappear when they tired of me. It wouldn't be hard either. Kill me, bury me and just say I had escaped.

So, yeah, my addiction to their hot sex would have to take a back seat to my addiction to wanting to live.

One morning, I noticed something was different about Dixon and Ashton as Ashton drove us to the apple orchard in the prison van. The two men were quieter than usual. Their bodies tense. Their gazes toward me lustier.

Something naughty was in the air and instinctively I knew today was the day when both of them would take me at the same time.

My pussy quivered and my ass clenched at the idea. I'd never been double penetrated before. Not by flesh and blood, well-hung men. I grew hot just thinking about it.

As I stepped out of the prison van, Dixon and Ashton, swooped in around me. Their eyes were bright with eagerness and their cocks impressively tented their pants. They were already aroused and so was I. My nipples felt bigger than usual, my pussy hung heavy and hot with need and my anal muscles were jerking around the plug with anticipation.

If I had my way, I'd have told them to take me right then and there, but I had other plans also circulating in my head for today.

"Today is the day," Dixon said, his blue eyes piercing me and making me tremble.

"We'll start right after lunch," Ashton replied in a giddy voice.

"Remove your plug during first break and then you'll be ready for both of us. We'll take you after lunch," Dixon instructed.

I nodded jerkily. My legs were jittery as I followed them to the apple orchard.

They removed my wrist and ankle chains and then Ashton placed the ankle monitor, reminding me that if I tried to take it off, or if I went more than a mile in any direction from them, the alarm would alert them as well as alert the prison.

Over the last few days, I'd discovered that Ashton used special tools to tighten the strap around the ankle bracelet and that he pushed a button on the little black box attached after securing it and before removing it. He kept the small tools that would remove the restraint in his breast pocket with the other keys.

I inhaled deeply as I gazed around the orchard and waited for Dixon and Ashton to bring me the first baskets full of apples so I could dump and sort them in the bin. Yup, there was still more work to be done. Still plenty of apples on the trees to be picked.

But today was *the* day.

Today, everything would come to a head.

Since deciding I would make an escape attempt I'd observed my two prison guards like my life depended on it. They were predictable and that would hopefully be their downfall and make my escape successful. Having a ménage before clearing out would be the icing on the cake, so to speak. It would be something to remember them by, just as a potential baby would be.

I smiled and resisted the urge to touch my abdomen. This baby, that is if I were pregnant, would be wanted by me even with it being an accident.

AT FIRST BREAK, THE men were exuberant in outlining what they planned to do to me after lunch and I had to admit I was seriously aroused and excited for them to take me. They agreed to work concessions and I behaved as if nothing was different. I knew that if I failed to escape, years would be added to my sentence, but if I didn't escape, I might be dead.

I really had no choice, did I?

Lunch couldn't come soon enough and when they presented me with a huge Chicken Caesar Salad sandwich, my mouth exploded with gratitude as I devoured the wonderful food.

I couldn't help but moan and groan my appreciation as the tangy flavors exploded against my tongue and made love to my taste buds. I noticed the two men would tense every time I made my noises, even though they sat twenty feet away eating and talking to each other in hushed tones.

Yup, they were definitely bisexual. Of that I had no doubt.

I also had no doubts that I would miss the sex.

My heart skipped a beat when lunch time was over and Dixon and Ashton walked over to me.

"Did you remove the plug as instructed?" Ashton asked.

"Yes, during break," I replied.

I don't know why he was asking as they'd watched me disappear during break after we'd worked out concessions. I'd walked a couple of rows over and done the deed, dropping the plug in a clump of tall grass beneath one of the apple trees that had already been picked clean. At this point I didn't care if the farmer or his helpers found it. Didn't care that it was unhygienic. Not my problem.

The only things on my mind had been my escape and the hot sex I'd be getting.

The two prison guards had done most of the work this morning, leaving me refreshed and ready to participate in a naughty little send off before I left for good.

The time had finally come for both.

"Get naked," Dixon instructed.

"You two get naked first. I want to watch a nice strip tease," I smiled inwardly at the surprise bursting in their eyes. Until now I'd been submissive during sex. Today, I'd trade things up.

"Okay," Ashton said slowly, a little amused smirk on his lips. He reached for his utility belt with weapons attached and unlatched it.

"You are the Queen," Dixon said and to my amusement, he bowed to me.

For a split second I had the intense feeling that these two men would never hurt or kill me. I clamped down on that unexpected feeling and concentrated on watching them.

Dixon removed his belt.

Excitement pulsed through me as they casually dropped their belts into the nearby tall grass. Their weapons would be easy to reach when the time came.

I licked my tongue teasingly along my lower lip, as I studied them. I made sure to smile and to lower my lashes prettily. May as well go out with a bang.

"Go on," I prodded.

They removed their radios, slowly placing them down on top of their belts.

I noted Ashton remove a tube of lube from his pant pocket. He tossed it onto the blanket near my feet.

"Nice, keep going," I encouraged.

My body was tightening with awareness as both men began to unzip their jackets. The jackets were placed upon their utility belts. Their shirts followed, revealing nicely toned muscles on the prison guards.

My breathing began to quicken as their hands slipped to the zippers on their pants. It was so cool how they both moved in unison, unzipping at the same speed as well-trained strippers. A moment later they both stepped out of their pants and tossed them onto the other clothing.

It didn't go unnoticed by me that they were piling everything upon their weapons, which would make it a bit lengthier to get at what I would need. My attention flew to their rock-hard looking erections pushing boldly against their underwear. I trembled at the sight. It would be in just a few short minutes before both of them took me.

Before they could lower their underwear, I stepped forward, reaching out my hands. I placed a palm on Dixon's hard hot chest and my other palm on Ashton's strong chest. Both men inhaled as I smoothed my hands over their curvy muscles. I found a nipple on each man and gently squeezed and pinched. Their buds beaded and grew hard.

They groaned their approval.

Then I lowered my head and sucked Ashton's hot nipple into my mouth. I suckled him. His hand came up and he grabbed hold of my upper arm and simply held on, panting as I tenderly bit his rigid flesh.

Then I moved over to Dixon's chest, sucking his beaded nipple into my mouth. He swore softly and reached up to cup my clothed breast. The heat from his hand torched me and he quickly found my nipple and began to squeeze and pinch until I was gasping. Ashton did the same, finding my nipple through the layers of clothing, pinching it and rubbing.

Before long I was moaning with pleasure as we all played with each other's nipples.

Man, I'd never done something so erotic before. It was crazy nice playing with men's nipples while they played with mine.

Soon, their hands were leaving my breasts and they began to undress me.

Tension grew inside me as Dixon unzipped my jumper.

The dominant expression on his face made me feel meek. His blue eyes looked stormy hot and my breaths came heavy and fast. I could feel my nipples swelling, and my breasts pushing hard against my top as the jumper was lowered to my waist. Dixon slid his hands under the hem of my top and then lifted. I raised my arms and he slipped my top over my head. He tossed the garment onto the pile of their clothes.

Cool autumn air breathed against my flesh, sending a chill into me. I shivered.

"Easy, we'll get you warm really fast," Ashton whispered from behind me.

He unclipped my bra at the back and it fell away, freeing my big breasts, baring them to Dixon. Appreciation made him smile. Instinctively I knew it was a genuine smile, something that came from deep within a part of him that valued big breasts. The tip of his tongue peeked out from between his lips, making me shiver with want.

"Steady yourself," Dixon instructed.

I grabbed his waist and held tight to him.

Dixon wasted no time. He cupped my breasts with his strong hands, warming me instantly. He lowered his head and his lips gingerly swept over mine in an intoxicating tease that had me whimpering at the onslaught of pleasurable tingles zipping around my mouth. My abdomen clenched as those naughty tingles arrowed down south, hitting my pussy with a big bang and making me cream hot juices.

Need slammed through me as Ashton stepped closer behind. His body heat warmed my backside and he pulled the jumper past my hips and then down my legs. I slid off my shoes and the jumper followed. Then Ashton's fingers dipped beneath the waistband of my pants and panties and he slid my clothing downward.

Despite feeling heady from Dixon's hot kisses, I managed to lift one leg and then the other so Ashton could get rid of the rest of my clothes.

By now I knew Dixon had a breast fetish and that Ashton had an ass fetish. I'd been told that Ashton would take me in the ass. So, it came as no surprise when the slurps of lube lashed through the air. Then his lubed finger caressed against my sphincter until I gave him access.

"She's nicely open back here. The plugs are worth their weight in gold," Ashton muttered.

Dixon didn't respond.

I inhaled sharply as Ashton began to press lube inside and against my eager anal muscles.

I could feel Dixon's big, clothed erection pushing against my lower abdomen. His flesh was a hot knot and his kisses burned my senses.

Chapter Twelve

Having both men touching me like this was whipping a whirlwind of anticipation through me.

Man, I wish I could stay here and get this wicked hot treatment from them every day.

My thoughts disintegrated as Dixon's fingers found my nipples and I moaned into his mouth as he brushed his thumbs over the sensitive tips in an agonizingly slow seduction. His kiss deepened and I bucked beneath the ravaging need inside my pussy as Dixon rubbed his package against me.

The rip of foil from behind had me tensing.

Condom time. Slurps of lube followed and I knew Ashton was lubing his shaft.

I tightened my grip on Dixon and moments later Ashton pushed his condom-sheathed engorged cockhead against my sphincter. I held my breath as he forced his cock deeper, penetrating and pushing his swollen shaft against my tender tissues.

The heat from his flesh was intense. The pressure of his impalement was incredibly beautiful bringing along a bite of pain. I'd never experienced something like this before. So hot in the ass. So big and all consuming. It was like I was being possessed.

Ashton withdrew and I moaned the loss into Dixon's mouth.

Dixon pressed his erection against my clitoris and I gasped as he gyrated there creating intense sensations that was quickly building toward an orgasm. He ripped his mouth away and began a bombardment of intoxicating kisses along my chin and then down the length of my neck, and across my chest.

I felt defenseless as Ashton held tight to my waist and plunged his cock into me again. I cried out at the impact. He withdrew and began a stroking rhythm that had me panting with his every hard thrust. There were so many incredible sensations smothering me. So much pleasure and bits of pain that destroyed my thoughts. I was trapped between their bodies. Lost and defenseless, but so enraptured.

Dixon's mouth captured my quivering nipple and more pleasure sang through me as he nipped and nibbled, licked and lapped. He backed off grinding against my clit and I could only sob with the sensations as Dixon's mouth made love to my nipples and Ashton pistoned his penis into my ass like he was a man possessed.

Dixon tore his mouth away from my nipple and uncupped my breasts. I let go of him and watched as his fingers glided beneath the waistband of his underwear. Then he slid them down over his hips and his cock sprang free, elongating and thickening like a giant snake.

Mercy, but his generous size always enthralled me.

His big cock bobbed as he stepped out of his underwear. Then he moved back in front of me, settling his palms upon my hips. I slapped my hands over his broad shoulders, loving the flexing of his muscles beneath my palms.

His expression was tight with exhilaration. His eyes flashed with heat and his face was flushed red.

"Your nipples are the best I've ever tasted," he complimented.

I couldn't even answer as Ashton pistoned into me again. I bucked and dug my fingernails into Dixon's shoulders, preventing myself from falling. Ashton pulled out and then thrust into me again, his cock strong and solid as my snug anus stretched around him in welcome. Then he withdrew.

Dixon quickly moved closer.

"Get ready for us, Queen," he whispered in a dark guttural voice that dazed my senses.

I moaned as in one wicked thrust Dixon had me impaled on his thick long penis. Somewhere deep in the back of my mind, something warned me to stop.

But I didn't pay attention.

I was already too hot, not wanting to break this mood. Besides all my self-control was gone as both men began an overwhelming thrusting.

In one went. Then out. In the other one went and then out.

The friction of two cocks seared my two intimate openings and I cried out at the bites of intoxicating pain and the shards of blissful pleasure. My thighs and lower belly tightened. My breaths came faster and faster.

I clamped my mouth over Dixon's mouth and thrust my tongue between his lips. He groaned as our tongues mated.

I moaned as their pistoning grew deeper and harder, their powerful bodies sandwiching me between them. Perspiration blossomed over my heated skin and slaps of their flesh pummelling me split through the air.

It didn't take long for me to come because of the earlier erotic stimulation upon my clitoris and nipples, and when I came, I came hard.

Pleasure shot through me like a scorching rocket. I went instinctual, bucking against Ashton, grinding against Dixon, and moaning into the tidal waves of pleasure.

The two prison guards gave me no mercy as they continued spearing their shafts into me. Over and over.

Sharp, hot convulsions pounded me. I twisted between the two men, moaning and whimpering as the exquisite pleasure made love to me. Their driving, profound strokes had me screaming and trembling as their solid heat filled me like I'd never been filled before.

It was so good. Too good.

My body throbbed. My pussy and ass clenched like vice grips around each impalement.

Dixon and Ashton just kept pistoning like a well-oiled machines. Never ending. Continuous.

And so were my orgasms.

I fought for breath as the climaxes consumed me. The pleasures shattered me, drowned me and carried me away to some faraway land where life *was* a climax. A world of pleasure and nothing else.

Sometime later, as I was slowly coming down from yet another wild orgasm, I heard Dixon and Ashton shout out their own releases. Felt heat from condom-captured sperm buried deep inside my ass from Ashton's cock. Jets of semen spurt within my vagina from Dixon. I suddenly realized why my mind had warned me to stop near the beginning.

Dixon hadn't been wearing a condom.

But it was too late anyway. So I just let my pussy milk him of his seed as I shuddered and convulsed and accepted what had happened yet again.

But it didn't really matter. I was pregnant anyway. My period hadn't come and I was always on schedule just like clockwork. Dixon had already put a baby in me.

Afterwards, no one spoke as we all lay down on the blanket, spent.

The warm autumn sunshine warmed our naked bodies and before long Ashton and Dixon were snoring with satisfied smiles on their faces.

Unfortunately, I had no time for languishing.

When I heard their breathing deepen and slow, I moved quickly yet quietly off the blanket. Gingerly I dressed in Ashton's prison guard uniform and slipped on his hat.

Then I buckled Ashton's heavy weapon laden belt around my waist. I grabbed Dixon's belt and both of the radios.

Holding my breath as fear pummelled me, I threw quick glances at the two sleeping prison guards and unbuttoned Ashton's shirt pocket. I located the two little tools that Ashton used to open and close my ankle monitor.

In a moment, the monitor dropped off my ankle and I pushed the button just like I'd seen Ashton do. I tossed the monitor off into the trees and then slipped my hand into the other breast pocket.

Shivers of both dread and excitement shot through me as I curled my fingers around the key to the van. I left the key there. For now.

I felt lightheaded with terror, despite being armed now, as I moved with the radios and weapons down the main row of apple trees to where we'd first started working this morning.

I dropped the items and picked up my ankle chains where they'd been left after Ashton had outfitted me with the ankle monitor. I left the wrist restraints and weapons there.

Despite my holding the ankle restraints gently and carefully in my hands, they still tinkled slightly. The noise zapped through the air like an explosion.

I froze. Had the guards heard?

I gazed down to where they lay on the blanket. Neither naked man moved.

My heart was beating so hard it felt like it was going to go through my chest as I began to move again and approached them.

I had to be crazy to be risking myself in hanging around here and doing what I was about to do to them, but I needed extra time to get away. I moved to their feet and crouched down.

I slid an open restraint under one of Dixon's ankles and clicked it shut, then with the other end, I cuffed Ashton's ankle. The two men were now cuffed naked to each other.

They continued to sleep.

Man, how lucky could I be?

I gave them one long last look as doubt crept into my mind. Should I leave or should I stay? No, I had to make a run for it. I'd be stupid to at least not try.

The sex had been good, but it was over.

Despite my wanting to run like a woman possessed, I tiptoed quietly once again back to where we'd started working this morning.

I gazed back. They continued to sleep.

For a brief moment regret flowed through me. They'd trusted me. Had figured I was too submissive to make a run for it.

They'd been wrong.

I shook away the regret, grabbed Dixon's weapon belt and the radios and slipped into the treeline.

Moments later I was at the van.

Exhilaration and an insane need to move fast raged through me. But despite my anxiety, I quietly opened the door and climbed into the driver's seat. I tossed the items onto the passenger seat, then slammed the key into the ignition and turned.

The engine rumbled to life.

Man, I hoped they didn't hear.

Slowly I turned the van around in the narrow farmer's lane. Soon, I was on my way.

I kept gazing into the rear-view mirror fully expecting to see them burst out of the trees and come running naked after me. But they were hobbled together. It would take them some time to figure out how to co-ordinate their walking while chained together.

It wouldn't be easy. I spoke from experience.

My foot kept pressing on the gas pedal and I kept having to ease off and slow down.

I had to act like I belonged in this vehicle. Like I was a prison guard. I yanked the cap lower on my head as I approached the dirt road that would lead to the highway. Thankfully, no one was around.

My knuckles were white as I held tight to the steering wheel. I felt woozy with fear. My legs were shaking and so was pretty much the rest of me.

I swear I almost passed out as I saw a black car whiz by just up ahead on the highway. When I came to the intersection, my mouth was so dry, that I could barely keep myself from stopping at the stop sign.

My heart crashed in my ears as I gazed left and then right. The other vehicle I'd seen was already way ahead in the distance.

I turned the van onto the highway, going the opposite way of the prison toward the city. Once I got to the city, I knew where to take it. To my old neighborhood. I'd remembered an acquaintance of my mom who knew someone who ran a chop shop.

I'll sell him the van and he'd make it disappear.

I grinned as I spied Dixon and Ashton's wallets in the tray between the seats. I knew someone who would give me a great deal of money for those radios, cop weapons, those wallets that would be filled with credit cards and ID. By the time Dixon and Ashton found help, I'd have hopped on a bus for another city in some new clothing purchased with cash.

I'd disappear.

I settled my hand upon my abdomen and smiled.

We were free.

The End

Taken by Two Lifeguards

Twenty-two-year-old professional swimmer and Olympic hopeful, Katie White, goes to the beach every day to continue work on her training by swimming in the ocean...and to do some secret naughty stuff on the side.

She also loves the lifeguard eye candy. Skimpy swim trunks on tanned muscular bodies put her in a really good mood. But the lifeguards don't seem to know she exists, especially after she broke up with her lifeguard boyfriend, Chad.

When Katie suddenly gets caught in a malicious storm, two lifeguards come to her rescue. One of them is Chad!

Stranded in the first-aid shack and being almost dead has made Katie awfully cold and her two lifeguard rescuers are going to warm Katie up nice and slow...

Copyright

Author Note

This is a work of fiction. Characters, places, settings, and events presented in this book are purely of the author's imagination and bear no resemblance to any actual person, living or dead or to any actual events, places, and/or settings.

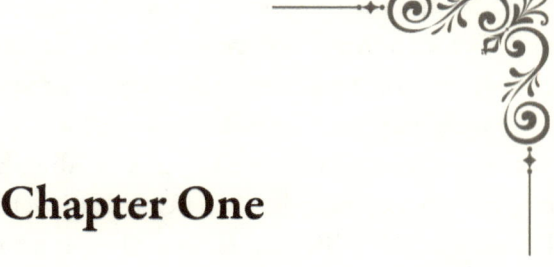

Chapter One

I'm always pretty tired after putting in a full day of swim training at the local gym, but I force myself to come to the beach every day just so I can relax and have some naughty private time. I've been professionally training as a swimmer for the Olympics since I was ten and I've rarely seen a sunrise unless the pool I'm training in has windows. My coach insists if I keep up with the weights, the workouts, yoga, hypoxic training and a bunch of other stuff, she will make sure I win gold at the next Olympics. She's been saying that since I can remember.

I'm twenty-two now and I've been close to winning on a few occasions but I'm getting older and I'm not so hopeful of winning gold anymore.

I've slowly come to realize that swimming professionally and winning competitions is not my vision. Instead, it is my grandmother's dream *for* me or more precisely, her dream for herself. She hadn't been able to achieve it because she'd been forced to marry at sixteen. She'd gotten pregnant and to avoid a family scandal, her parents had pushed her to marry the guy who'd knocked her up. A few months later, my dad was born.

My grandmother has been my primary caretaker since I was nine. That's when my parents died in a car crash. I've been swimming since then, to please her.

Grandpa died suddenly a few years ago of a massive heart attack and I've continued to live with her because I can't afford living elsewhere while I train, so I take care of her when I'm at home.

Lately though, I've been looking for every excuse under the sun not to go home. I just feel trapped; feeding her mashed up food and emptying her commode when her arthritis acts up and she can't care for herself just isn't a life goal for me. She has a bad habit of guilt tripping me into caring for her, saying that she took care of my sorry ass for many years and now it's my turn to give back.

The highlight of my day is coming here to the beach to get away from everything.

The lifeguard eye candy is a bonus. Hot, tanned muscles on very tall, lean men wearing skimpy swim trunks make my pulse and pussy react. For the longest time, those handsome hunks had been off limits for a shy girl like me, but one of them had asked me out earlier this summer and I'd said yes.

We were together for awhile, but we aren't anymore. He works here as a lifeguard and no other guy has asked me out since our breakup.

I also love the scenic short drive along the California coastline to get here. The hills are filled with expensive mansions on one side of the highway and on the other side there's white sandy beaches and dark blue ocean. For the longest time, I thought when I made it big at the Olympics I would buy one of those big houses. It would be better than living in that rat trap, one bedroom apartment with grandma.

But now I'm thinking of quitting grandma's dream and getting a good paying job, moving out and just figuring out what to do with the rest of my life. For sure, I'd still come here to the beach.

The sight of those hunky lifeguards sitting on their perches, their big muscles tense and their bodies fully alert and ready to tackle a potential drowning, always gets me into a mood to masturbate. That's another reason I come here, so I can swim out to the unmanned lighthouse miles down the coast and spend some quality time with myself.

I parked my car in the almost empty parking lot and wondered where everyone was today. As usual the late summer sun was bright, not a cloud in the sky and yet there was just a handful of vehicles nearby. I liked it better with lots of people. It gave me the opportunity to become a wallflower and just disappear into the ocean without one of the lifeguards watching me.

Oh well, I'd just stick to my routine.

I stuffed my wallet into the glove compartment, grabbed my towel, snapped my car key onto my necklace and got out of the car. The heat blasted against me like a furnace and I inhaled the salty air. I gazed along the beach, hoping my ex-boyfriend wasn't here today. It was awkward with him around, especially in the way things had ended between us.

I'd already changed into my swimsuit back at the gym, and I wore my white terrycloth robe and sandals as I strolled to the beach. There was one lifeguard perched on his lookout, but he was too far away for me to see who it might be and thankfully I was going the opposite way.

I was one of those shy young women who really didn't know how to talk to men. That's why I'd been surprised when Chad, a lifeguard, had taken an interest in me and we'd started dating.

But when I'd seen him and another lifeguard coming out of the first aid shack with one of those cute flirty blonde surfer girls who always hung around them, I knew *something* had been going on. I'd heard the rumors. Sometimes one or two or even three lifeguards would disappear in that shack for awhile with a female and the girl always came out with a big smile on her face.

Sometimes I wished I were one of those girls. But it was just a naughty fantasy that I toyed with in being with more than one guy at the same time. I was a good girl. Raised that way by my strict God-fearing grandmother. That's probably why my cheeks always went red when a guy talked to me. Even my ex, Chad, had commented on that issue.

Chad took night courses at the local college. He was going to be an electrician. It would be a decent job for him and I had thought he would be a good man for me. Oh well, I was twenty-two years old and I had no prospects of settling down with a guy that had future written all over him anyways, so why bother thinking about it.

In my opinion I wasn't Chad's equal in the take home pay department because I'd spent all my time training, instead of getting an education that would get me a well-paying job for my future.

Once again, I had my old fashion grandmother to blame, and of course, myself. Any winnings from competitions went back into the coach's salary and food and rent for us, instead of college courses. She expected me to marry some rich guy, but that wasn't going to happen because the last thing I wanted was to be dependant on a man for my shelter and food, like she'd been.

"Don't give away your milk, unless the farmer puts a ring on your finger," she'd say.

Damn hypocrite.

So, yeah, she thought I was still a virgin. But I wasn't. Tall, dark and dreamy Chad Samson had taken care of that on our second date and I'd loved it!

I found a secluded spot on the beach behind some high dunes and lay my towel down in the nice warm sand. Then I slipped off my sandals and robe and placed them neatly beside the towel. I wanted to portray the illusion that I was coming back soon. I removed my necklace with car key on it and slid it beneath the sand under the towel. I doubted anyone would even want to steal my old car that broke down every other week. They'd be doing me a favor if they did take it!

I walked toward the crashing breakers and noticed the surf was pretty rough with curling whitecaps. There were a string of screaming surfer girls catching the waves, but they didn't pay attention to me.

Several of the lifeguard perches remained empty and I figured I knew where those guys were. In the first aid shack with one or two of those surfer girls.

What pleasures went on in that hut anyway? I'd be interested in finding out.

Maybe I shouldn't have freaked out on Chad after spying him coming out of there with another lifeguard and a girl several weeks ago. When I told him I'd seen him, he'd gotten so pissed off saying if I'd have sex with him more often then he wouldn't have to look elsewhere. So, I'd told him to go right ahead and look elsewhere!

But I missed him. Missed his sweet smile and the twinkling of his brown eyes.

His endearing dream for me was for me to get out from under my grandmother's control.

The things I missed the most about him though, were his six pack abs, the gorgeous velvet-encased hard-as-a-rock mushroom-shaped cockhead that he'd taught me to take into my mouth and the forceful way his thick shaft made love to my quaking pussy, penetrating deep into my vagina until I was gasping from the fullness of his hard flesh and trembling from his scorching heat.

I blew out a tense breath as my pussy quivered with a need to be penetrated. I ran toward the roaring surf, trying to push Chad and my jealousy out of my mind.

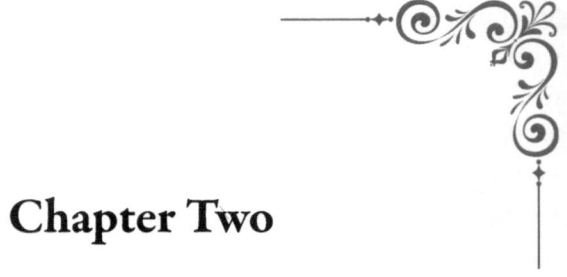

Chapter Two

I jumped into the mild water, loving how it splashed forcefully against me.

Quickly, I walked further into the ocean until the water touched my hot, throbbing pussy.

The seductive back and forth caresses of the surf against my swollen clitoris had me gasping. I wished I could reach down and slip my fingers into my bikini bottom and rub my sensitive clit and make myself come. But I was out in the open. Someone could be watching.

I gazed up the beach where I could see my little target. The lighthouse perched on a spit, accessible only by water because they always kept the fifteen-foot-high chain link gate locked to prevent trespassers from hanging out there.

I held my breath and dove into the water, embracing the wet liquid engulfing my entire body. I swam underwater for as long as I could hold my breath before surfacing. The hot sun beat down on my head and face, but the rest of me was immersed in cool fluid.

I got into my synchronized swimming very quickly. My arms sliced through the water with ease, and I enjoyed getting the kinks out of my calf muscles by kicking my legs. I swam with my focus entirely on the lighthouse several miles away.

White waves curled around me trying to drag me under and salty water slapped against my face, pissing me off and yet I kept swimming. I was used to the challenges of the ocean. And the powerful roar of the surf crashing against the nearby beach empowered me.

I swam faster.

By the time I reached the sandy beach in front of the lighthouse, I felt invigorated, my body primed for some naughty alone time action.

Ocean water sluiced off my skin as I stepped onto the sunny beach. The hot sun pummelled my wet body and the scorching sand slipped between my tender toes while I walked around the base of the building. I knew the lighthouse was unmanned and after a quick exploration to confirm I was alone; I smiled and quickly removed my bikini top.

I gazed down the coastline to where I'd left my towel and sandals and noted the handful of people on the beach were the size of ants. I inhaled deeply and watched my breasts jiggle and jut with appreciation at being out and free. The hot sun pummelled my flesh and the wicked wind lapped at my nipples, caressing and arousing them until they were hard peaks.

Then I moved to the side of the lighthouse where I sat down on the soft bed of cool green moss that grew in the shade of the towering building and examined my pert breasts.

I like my breasts. They're not too big and not too small and they fit perfectly in Chad's palms. Sexual tension smoldered through me as I thought about him. He's six feet tall compared to my five feet five. And he has the softest lips. But maybe all guys had soft lips? I didn't know, as Chad was the only guy I'd ever kissed.

I inhaled deeply as I cupped my cool smooth mounds the way Chad used to do. He'd squeeze them gently, testing their weight and then his head would lower and he'd suck a nipple into his hot mouth, creating shivery sensations as he licked and nibbled.

Excitement roared through me as I pinched and pulled at my pink nipples whipping up an awesome throbbing pleasure pain that had me gasping at the intensity. Between my thighs I felt the warm cream of arousal seeping out of me.

Then I slipped out of my bikini briefs and lay on my back upon the soft moss. With one hand, I kept seductively smoothing my palm over my breasts, tweaking and pulling my nipples, relishing the pleasure which arrowed from my breasts to between my legs.

I lifted my knees and spread my legs, then slipped one hand between my thighs, moaning as my fingers found my hot engorged clitoris.

Slowly, softly, I began rubbing at the tight, sensitive bundle of nerves until pleasure quivered and more hot cream poured into my vagina.

Then I dipped a finger inside my channel, collecting my wetness, bringing out my cream and using it as lube as I massaged my tender clit.

I rubbed my clit harder, creating a yummy friction. Dipped my fingers between my soft labia folds and into my vagina to gather more hot cream. Then I massaged my swollen, wet clitoris harder and harder. Fiery need gripped me. I tweaked my nipples until they were solid pebbles and on fire with pleasure and pain.

My breath caught as tension consumed me. Sensitive nerve endings fired deep within and my pussy, my belly and my breasts tightened. My vagina clenched and I rapidly pistoned my finger into my channel like it was a mini-cock on a mission.

I rubbed my breasts until my body ached.

The orgasm neared, my breaths came faster and then my self-control snapped. Instinctively I arched my hips and cried out as lashes of pleasure thrashed me.

I went manic, gyrating my hips, thrusting two fingers into my vagina and soared toward ecstasy. Convulsions gripped me and I gasped as I rode the deep, penetrating contractions.

I cried out as my release overwhelmed me and spun me into the wonderous world of pleasure I craved so much since Chad had introduced me to it.

My vagina spasmed and my ass tightened as the driving pleasure roared through me. It was never ending and I loved sailing within the spasms. Finally the shudders ebbed, and I lay on the beach panting, my naked body dotted with perspiration.

I longed to reach out and slip into my bikini top and bottom, but I ignored the impulse. I simply wanted to languish here in the aftereffects of my orgasm, enjoying the brisk, hot wind as it kissed every part of my exposed flesh.

Lying here, fully exposed, was heaven and pure peace.

I listened to the crying seagulls as they sailed overhead and heard the pounding surf roar onto the beach mere feet away. The nature sounds were my lullaby. An ocean song of freedom that lulled me to sleep.

I dreamed of nothing. Didn't want to. This was my special time away from everything.

No coach. No grandma. No two-timing ex-boyfriend who hadn't even thought that *maybe* I might want to be invited into that first-aid shack with him and another lifeguard.

No, nothing.

It was nice, black, and calm. I slept deep. Really deep, loving the relaxation and I didn't come awake until I heard the ominous rumble of thunder as it echoed all around me with a warning force.

Oh, crap!

I opened my eyes and stared up into the sky. No longer was it a happy clear brilliant baby blue, but now there were low hanging gun-metal gray-colored billows gazing down at me. I gasped as silver lightning forked out of the rolling clouds and into the nearby ocean.

Adrenaline seared through me as I scrutinised the area where I'd left my towel, sandals and car keys.

Dread hollowed out my tummy. I couldn't see the coastline beneath the silvery sheets of rain that were speeding toward me. For a split second, I thought about hunkering down here and waiting out the storm, but there was no overhang on the lighthouse to protect me from the rain.

Panic snapped through me and I quickly donned my bikini. Then, without hesitation, I dove into the water.

Immediately, I realized I was in trouble. The wind had picked up big time while I'd languished and the waves were powerfully rough as they curled over me with ominous force. Despite my nap, it appeared I wasn't as refreshed as I should have been, but hell, I wasn't going to spend the night out here.

Besides, Grandma would freak out having her slave gone missing!

My mouth went dry with fear as the tumultuous waves literally picked me up and rolled me up and toward the sea.

Oh man! Come on! Give me a break!

I forced every ounce of my energy into fighting the waves. I just needed to swim to the shoreline, then I could walk back to my car.

Desperation gripped me as another wave curled over me like a giant arm. I held my breath as it pulled me under. Terror made me kick my feet and swim like a mad woman until my head burst through the choppy surface.

I dragged in a deep breath, inhaling the rain-streaked salty air.

Shit! That was close!

Thunder crashed overhead and bright flashes of lightning reassured me I was still alive.

But for how long?

I pushed my fear and despair from my mind. Forced myself to concentrate with my entire being into doing what needed doing, which was staying alive and swimming back to shore.

I didn't know how long I swam. Didn't even know I was going the right way, but my arms began cramping and my legs felt floppy. I kept sinking into the quietness beneath the ocean and every time I managed to break to the surface, the roar of the waves and crackles of thunder made me think about going back under where it was quiet.

Water kept smashing against my face and it was getting harder to breathe. My eyes burned from the salt water and I could barely see.

Slowly my thoughts turned to giving up.

Just give up, Katie. Open your mouth and let the water in. Just go limp. It'll be over soon.

Just then something hard and orange nudged against my shoulder. I heard a shout. A man yelling to grab hold to the life preserver.

Huh? I must be hallucinating. I could only see the big waves crashing into my face. Another black wave rolled over me. I swallowed salt water. Coughed. Swallowed more.

Shit!

I was going to give up. I had no choice.

Another giant wave curled over me and swallowed me. I just held my breath and went under. I became limp. All my fight was gone. It was time to die.

I envisioned myself as a ragdoll just flopping around in the sea. I couldn't hold my breath anymore, and for a second I was terrified as the water seeped into me.

This is it. I'm dead.

Then suddenly, I felt very calm as the breath was sucked out of me. So calm.

Everything went black.

Chapter Three

"She's coming around," I heard a man's voice echo in my ears as I puked up the bitter salty water I'd inhaled and swallowed.

Man, I felt bad. My throat was on fire and my nostrils burned. And I was terribly cold. I couldn't stop shivering. My teeth were chattering a mile a minute too.

"She's hypothermic. We need to get her to the shack and out of that bikini and slowly warm her up," a familiar man's voice replied.

I recognized it instantly.

Oh crap. My ex-boyfriend, Chad.

I felt myself being lifted and then carried. Rain pelted my cold face, but I didn't care. For awhile I just listened to the roar of the surf, the crash of the thunder and then it suddenly got quieter. A moment later I was being lowered onto something soft.

I opened my eyes. They burned because of the salt water I'd been in, but I could see him clearly and my tummy somersaulted in a nice kind of way. He looked so hot in the way he gazed at me with such concern in his brown eyes.

Why in the world had I broke up with him again? My mind whirled with that question as I stared at him and appraised his features.

His medium-length sandy brown hair was wet and slicked back off his face just as always. I'd admired the fact that all he had to do was smooth a hand over his hair and push it back off his forehead and it would stay that way.

He was nicely tanned from the sun and he was broad shouldered with slim hips. He wore my favorite black Speedo bathing suit which illuminated the outline of his large shaft.

I could hear scissors snipping and I looked to my right to see Chad was cutting one bikini strap and then the other one. I felt my ice-cold skimpy top being removed, exposing my chilled breasts to him.

"Nice breasts," I heard a man say.

Surprisingly, my cheeks warmed at his compliment.

"Shut up, Stretch. That's unprofessional and she's awake," Chad replied tartly.

"Get off her bottoms too," came Stretch's voice.

As far as I could tell, there were just the two of them in the small building. From the several life preservers hanging on a nearby wall and several metal shelves filled with first aid stuff, I figured I was in the lifeguards' first aid shack. This was the shack the men took the flirty surfer girls to. The same shack I'd seen Chad and another lifeguard coming out of with one of those chicks.

And here I had almost drowned to get the luxury of seeing inside this building.

I heard the scissors snipping and felt my bottoms being removed.

Then a fluffy blanket covered me. But I still felt awfully cold.

"When is this storm going to let up?" I heard Stretch murmur. He'd moved to the lone window and was gazing out. Rivulets of rain ran down the glass and it was pretty dark outside.

"Anyone out there?" Chad asked as he placed two hot fingers to my wrist. He was checking my pulse.

"There're only three cars left. Yours, mine and Katie's. But we can't get out though."

"Why not?" Chad's head snapped up and he frowned at Stretch.

"Because I can see from here the road is washed away and there's a river running right through it. The landline is out and my cell phone doesn't work, so unless yours is working, she's our patient now."

"I left mine at home this morning. Forgot to charge it last night and was in too much of a hurry to look for the charger and bring it with me."

"Yeah, great. Well it's her fault we're still here," Stretch complained.

Chad shook his head and rolled his eyes.

"Had you not been watching her masturbating through your damn high-tech binoculars, like you always do, I'd be home making supper."

Oh my goodness! Chad had been watching me?

I should be embarrassed, but surprisingly I wasn't. Maybe the hypothermia was making me not care?

I noticed his cheeks redden and I couldn't help but let out a little giggle. He'd made fun of my red cheeks and now he was blushing himself!

"Yeah, and had I not been watching her, she'd be dead now, wouldn't she?" Chad snapped. Anger laced his voice and I was glad he was sticking up for me.

"How are you feeling??" Chad asked as he caught me watching him.

"Still c-c-old. Ice-c-c-old." I replied through chattering teeth.

"Don't we have any more emergency blankets?" Chad growled.

"You're the one who orders stuff and you were on vacation. I told you, before you left we needed some because someone broke in and stole the few we had left."

Chad inhaled deeply as if trying to calm himself.

"They were ordered and should have been here by now," he said in a tight voice.

Stretch moved away from the window and came closer. I caught him watching me.

"Do you have any blankets or clothes in your car, Katie?" Stretch asked.

I shook my head.

"I d-don't like being this c-cold," I complained.

A tinge of panic rippled through me. What if I never got warm again? I couldn't live like this!

Chad nodded, and he was biting on his lower lip. I knew he was thinking. Formulating a plan. He always worried his bottom lip when he was planning something.

"The only alternative is sandwiching her between us. Use our body heat to warm her," Chad said in a hoarse voice.

Stretch made a strangled laugh.

"A manwich? With your ex?"

"Come on. Let's be quick. She needs to get warmed up. You'll have to lose your wet swimsuit."

Stretch cursed and shook his head.

I frowned, wondering what his problem might be.

"Come on, man. You know how I am around naked ladies," Stretch complained.

"She's seen an erection before. Just control yourself." Chad said.

I smiled. At least I think I did. I watched Chad strip off his tight bathing suit. My eyes widened and my cold pussy shivered with a spark of heat as I saw his giant penis.

Oh my goodness, I remembered his cock quite well. From the two-inch wide girth that fit me so well, to the thick blue veins that interlaced the entire velvet-encased eight-inch hard length that held his scrumptious purplish mushroom-shaped cockhead.

Awareness began to melt that godawful cold that was clinging to me like a bad virus. Chad stood beside me where I lay on a sheet-covered mattress which made me wonder why they hadn't covered me with the sheet.

Heck, if the blanket wasn't warming me, then I figure the sheet wouldn't do the job either. Movement caught my gaze from my left side and I turned my head to watch Stretch lowering his tight bathing suit.

I held my breath as his giant serpent of a cock uncurled and stuck straight out like a steel pole and it was flushed red with excitement.

Obviously seeing my naked breasts moments earlier had turned him on.

Big time. `

Stretch's cock was a bit shorter than Chad's but much thicker. And I detected a glisten of pre-cum at the tip of his plum-shaped cockhead. Now I understood his complaint. It appeared he got quite aroused on seeing a naked woman, even one who'd almost died.

But hey, I could forgive him for his arousal. I must be an attractive woman. Until now, I hadn't really thought of myself in that way.

Both men were extraordinarily well-endowed and something naughty and hot quivered deep inside my lower belly at the sight of two juicy shafts.

I liked this heat. Wanted to explore it. Needed more of it.

Suddenly I knew if I could claim this passion burning deep inside of me, then I would be able to kill off my good-girl innocence and truly embrace my true self. My brush with death would turn me into a woman who wanted to expose herself to all things sexual.

I could feel my heart begin to beat faster as Chad lifted the blanket. The mattress moved as he slid his hot body in beside me.

"Come on. Turn on your side toward me. This will work better if we snuggle nice and close like we used to," Chad said. His voice sounded thick and hoarse.

Geez. I had to be practically dead before the man decided to pay attention to me again.

I nodded and bit back a sudden swell of emotions as I remembered the two of us in his tiny apartment, lying on his sofa bed, snuggled in each other's arms with barely enough room for us on the mattress.

Just like now.

I scooted close to him and heard him exhale as our bodies touched. His face was mere inches from my face and I relished the warm air of his breath caressing my cheeks. His hot legs pushed against mine and his boiling chest pressed against my breasts, but he kept his lower half from touching me. Despite that, I enjoyed his body heat wafting between the few inches separating our bodies.

"You're like an iceberg," Chad said.

"Feel like one too," I admitted.

My, oh, my, he was so nice and warm. I resisted the impulse to reach out and wrap my arms around his waist.

Chad looked over my shoulder.

"Come on, Stretch. Get your ass over here."

"Coming," he grumbled behind me.

Awareness of having a strange man seeing me naked made me tense as the blanket lifted behind me. The mattress moved as Stretch climbed in. He pushed his hot body against mine, lining up his legs against the back of mine, his upper torso against my back and I softly inhaled as the outline of his scorching shaft pressed against the curve of my upper ass cheek.

Chapter Four

"**N**ice and toasty," I whispered as Stretch's body heat slammed into me.

I could hear the men's breaths quickening. Could feel Stretch's shaft growing larger. I could also feel my ass clenching as I imagined Stretch sliding his cock into me there.

I swallowed as my body tensed.

Chad had closed his eyes, and for several minutes I thought he might have fallen asleep, until he spoke.

"I noticed you aren't trembling as much. Are you feeling better?" he asked.

He'd opened his eyes and his brown gaze was hooded and filled with lust.

"Much better, but still pretty cold," I complained. I didn't want them to move away. I enjoyed feeling two strong male bodies pressed in around me like a *manwich*, using the term Stretch had mentioned earlier.

Chad nodded and fell silent.

Rain pounded against the roof of the shack and flashes of lightning flickered at the lone window. Thunder boomed. It appeared the storm wasn't going anywhere. Neither was the hot need brewing inside of me.

"There is an ancient saying that when you save someone's life, you own them," Stretch murmured. His face touched the back of my head and I could feel his hot breath against my neck. I liked the warmth and the feel of their flesh upon mine.

"Quiet, Stretch. Let her recuperate," Chad broke in.

Stretch had hit on something. I would be dead if they hadn't rescued me. I would be that limp rag doll I had imagined being tossed around out there in the waves. I would be dead meat. Shark food. And I would not even have experienced life.

Or lived my sexual fantasies.

And I wanted to live one of them. Having sex with my ex and with another man at the same time.

And I wanted to do it right now.

I shivered as a cold wave of dread overwhelmed me.

Oh, man, suddenly it felt like life was way too short for everything that I wanted to do, sexually.

"Are you okay?" Chad asked.

I opened my eyes. He was still staring at me and my pussy trembled as I decided on something.

"I-I think. There is a way for you b-both to make me feel really h-hot," I whispered.

Chad grinned. "Oh yeah? What's that? If you want some hot chocolate, the power is out, so I can't boil you up some."

Silly man. Hot chocolate was for kids. And what part of *both of them* didn't he get?

"Make love to me," I said.

Oh, my goodness! Had I said that out loud?

In the enjoyable manner that Stretch tensed against me and the stunned way Chad was staring at me made me realize that yes, I had said my request out loud.

From behind me, Stretch cursed softly beneath his breath.

Chad appeared to recover quickly, his facial expression going stoic.

"That certainly would warm you up, but with hypothermia your core needs to be warmed slowly or you could go into cardiac arrest or organ failure," Chad explained.

Seriously? I was wanting sex and he was offering me an explanation as to why not?

Frustration grabbed a hold of me. Perhaps this man was way too serious for me. Maybe I had been all wrong about him having future written all over him? Did I really need to spell it out to him?

"So, be inventive. Warm me up slowly. Both of you."

Against my ear, Stretch cursed again.

Chad's Adams apple bobbed in his throat as he stared at me.

"You're under duress. You're not thinking clearly. It's unprofessional." Chad murmured.

"I've never thought more clearly. I want to know what those surfer girls experience when they come into this shack."

"You heard the lady," Stretch said with a chuckle.

I didn't push him away as his hot hand slid over my shoulder and he cupped my left breast. His palm scorched my cold flesh. I gasped as he began pinching my nipple. At first it felt painful, foreign. But then my nipple responded.

It elongated, felt bigger. Pleasure mingled with sultry pain.

A nice feeling erupted between my thighs. I felt wet and hot down there as my pussy lips engorged and warm cream seeped down my vagina.

Stretch's movements made the blanket lower and Chad's eyes grew wider as he watched what Stretch was doing to me.

"Katie…" Chad hissed. His voice sounded strangled, unsure.

"Shh, I know what I want. Kiss me. Kiss me all over," I demanded.

I trembled with excitement.

Doubt flooded his eyes. Nice, sexy brown eyes. I'd never gotten enough of looking into them.

"Pretend I'm one of those girls," I whispered.

I wanted this. Yet he hesitated. I could imagine what he was thinking. Screw her brains out so she'll live or keep her as a manwich filling until they could get out of here and make her suffer the cold that was still invading her body.

"No strings," I added for incentive.

"I've got condoms and lube right here in the drawer," Stretch murmured against my neck.

I nodded.

"Get them," I instructed. My voice sounded bold, determined. Aroused.

Stretch's hand slid off my breast and he turned away but didn't get out of bed. A second later, I heard a drawer slide open.

"She's a virgin back there," Chad protested.

"I'll go easy on her," he said hoarsely.

I could tell Chad was finally getting enthusiastic in the way his nostrils flared as he looked at me like a predator about to get something he wanted.

A rip of foil snapped through the air. I could hear Stretch sliding on a condom and then the slurp of lube. Juicy sounds ripped through the air as he massaged the lube onto his cock.

"Reach back and take me inside of you," Stretch growled as he once again stretched out behind me.

I bit my bottom lip and did as he asked.

I moved my arm back and down and quickly felt his swollen shaft throbbing against my palm.

I wrapped my fingers around his solid, pulsing flesh and angled it toward my ass.

I gasped at the awesome feel of his smooth plum-shaped cockhead as I pressed it against the tight circle of muscles and nerves around my anal opening.

STRETCH HISSED AND I trembled and gasped as I pushed the tip of his scorching cockhead into me.

He was big and swollen and my anal canal felt so tight and protested the invasion by clenching around him.

"That's it, Katie. We'll do this nice and slow," Stretch murmured against my ear.

His arm slid over my shoulder once more and he cupped my breast with his palm. His strong fingers tweaked and pulled my nipples until my pussy and ass tightened with naughty need.

"Your turn," I whispered to Chad who had been watching my reaction at having another man's penis pushing into my behind.

"Are you sure you want this?" Chad asked. His eyes blazed with heat and I found myself responding.

I nodded jerkily.

At the moment there was nothing more that I wanted. Especially figuring I should be dead.

"We do this slow. So her core warms slowly. Got it?" Chad said as he looked over my shoulder and appeared to hold Stretch's gaze with warning.

"I know how to warm up a woman nice and slow, my man. I wasn't born yesterday."

Chad nodded and I shuddered as his hand settled on my hip. His calloused fingers began to knead my cold flesh there.

He drew his face closer to me, his warm breath caressing my chilled cheeks. Then his hot mouth melted over my trembling lips in a soft, heated kiss. I moaned my appreciation as pleasure whipped through me and he deepened the kiss.

The sound of my moan must have turned Stretch on even more as his cock nudged into me another inch. His partially buried, lubed shaft felt oh-so-big and I closed my eyes against the burst of pleasure pain as his hard flesh throbbed inside me.

Thankfully, he didn't move deeper. He must have sensed I needed time to get used to his penetration.

Chad's mouth became more forceful capturing my attention. His teeth nipped at my lower lip, creating pinpricks of seductive pain. And then he licked my bruised flesh, soothing the fire he'd created. He slipped his tongue past my lips and boldly pushed into my mouth to duel with my tongue.

The impact made me heady.

Chad's hand slipped beneath my other breast. He began massaging me there as he drew me deeper into his kiss, then he pinched and pulled on my nipple much in the same way Stretch continued to do at my other breast.

I sank into the pleasure both men created. The icy grip claiming my core released and thankfully I began to warm.

I welcomed the hotness. Oh, how I welcomed it.

Boldly, I pulled on Stretch's solid penis, encouraging him to penetrate me deeper. I wanted his heat searing into me, claiming me, possessing me.

I gasped into Chad's mouth as Stretch pushed his cock in another inch.

Hot fire penetrated my ass and my anal muscles protested and clamped tight around his flesh. The pressure was intense and I wasn't sure if I could go on but Stretch breathed softly against my ear and sucked on my earlobe creating an uncontrollable trembling in my shoulders and an erotic clenching of my vagina.

With my free hand, I found Chad's erection. His hot flesh pulsed and jerked as I wrapped my palm and fingers around the thick base and held his throbbing shaft.

In response, Chad's tongue shot into my mouth like a heat seeking missile, making my hands automatically tighten around both of the men's rock-hard throbbing flesh.

Stretch's lips let go of my ear lobe and slowly he slid his mouth along the back of my neck, pressing delicate kisses that had me arching, which made his penis plunge even deeper.

I yelped at the pleasure pain as the pressure became so intense and so blistering hot, I was moaning and writhing between the two lifeguards.

Chad broke the kiss and his face moved lower, his lips kissing my chin and then butterfly kisses along my neck that had me shuddering. I watched as he nudged Stretch's hand from my breast and then Chad's hot lips greedily circled my nipple. He began to suck, drawing on my throbbing bud like a man possessed.

Fire raged through my core as male hands seductively massaged along the curve of my hip and along my abdomen. I loved how their touches chased away the icy cold, leaving me feeling almost normal again.

Well, normal isn't the right word. Feverish with desire. Needy. Desperate for a more intimate contact. Urgent to have the fire of both men's cocks buried deep inside of me.

"I need more. Give me more," I pleaded.

I felt Stretch's hand curl over my shoulder and he gently squeezed.

"Consider me your personal butt plug, beauty. Now trust me on what happens next and stay relaxed," he whispered against my neck.

I didn't know what he meant until he suddenly rolled me halfway on top of him and I cried out as his shaft pierced deeper. Bites of pleasure pain seared into me and the pressure grew so intense I thought for sure Stretch was going to split my behind in two!

Chapter Five

The foreign feeling of heaviness eased and the panic of his fullness had me frantically gasping for breaths. That he was now buried deep inside me had me closing my eyes and willing myself to remain calm as my anal muscles happily spasmed around his sizzling flesh.

"I love the way your ass makes love to my cock," Stretch breathed as he nibbled on my earlobe.

Instinctively I turned my head making him let go of my earlobe and I caught his lips in a kiss. He groaned and kissed me back, his mouth branding my senses and sending shockwaves of pleasure through me.

Suddenly I was riding a wave of high. I wanted to lose myself in a frenzy of pleasure.

As I frantically kissed him I could feel his long, thick shaft vibrating inside me. It was thickening and elongating, stretching deeper. Somewhere in the back of my mind I wondered if that's why they called him Stretch, because he certainly was stretching into my ass.

Now I realized why he'd moved me into this new pose. I was literally impaled on his cock, unable to escape, not that I wanted to, but with this new position I was also fully frontally exposed for Chad.

Chad had easier access to me and he was certainly entertaining himself with my breasts.

His hands were massaging my mounds and he was licking and sucking on one nipple until it was a throbbing mass before he moved his mouth to my other nipple. He pleasured me alternately with his tongue and his teeth, lapping and nipping until my nipple was so hot I could hardly stand the splintering mix of pleasure and pain.

Blindly, I found and then slid my hands upon his muscular chest and was about to push him away because his mouth was becoming so intense, but before I could, he let go of my tender nipple with a loud pop.

His head went lower. My hands fell off his chest and I curled my fingers against the back of his neck.

As Stretch's kiss deepened, I became intoxicated with desire. A hunger for more intimacy was bursting inside me.

Chad's lips moved over my quivering abdomen in mind destroying kisses that had me automatically lifting my left leg. Quickly, I settled it over his muscular shoulder, giving him full access to the intimate zone between my thighs.

As Chad's mouth drew closer to my pussy, I broke the kiss with Stretch and watched Chad with anticipation. During our short time together in our relationship, I had never allowed him to do oral. Had never allowed him to so much as look at my pussy, even when we'd been having sex.

Blame it on my good girl upbringing, But now, I craved him.

I tensed as his face lowered between my thighs.

I whimpered as I waited, filled with awe as his breath caressed my pussy lips. I tried to pull his head forward, but he was like iron. Steadfast.

"Easy Katie, let me look at your pussy," he breathed.

I watched his face. It was lit up with appreciation, a wonderous smile on his mouth. Even his brown eyes glittered with gratitude.

"So damn beautiful. So perfect. Never be afraid of showing a man or a woman your succulent pussy, Katie. Now that I've seen it, I don't think I will ever have enough of looking at it," he whispered.

I was stunned at his words and realized I would never have heard them had I drowned. Something inside of me shifted. My deep-down inner shyness completely disintegrated, replaced with a feeling of daring, and an emotion of wanting to be naughty.

Never again would I be ashamed of my intimate body parts. Screw grandma and her old-fashioned restraints.

The intoxicating way Chad was looking at the apex of my thighs, exhilarated me and I wanted my sexual freedom. I wanted to be just like those surfer girls I envied!

Chad lowered his head and I moaned as his lips tenderly sucked on my labia lips.

A savage need was building in me with lightning speed. My abdominal muscles were tightening and I cried out as Chad lapped luxuriously at my ultra-sensitive clitoris. His tongue was like a whip-master, lashing back and forth, up and down, around and around, until my clit was fever hot and so sensitive that I knew I would climax at any second.

My thighs felt rock-hard and my ass muscles were wrapped ultra-tight around Stretch's big cock.

Every muscle in my body was primed, every nerve ending igniting, sparking, fighting for release. I was aching, and in a really good way.

Stretch was groaning beneath me and Chad was moaning as he continued to play with my clit drawing me closer and closer to the edge of bliss.

Prickling heat and perspiration skipped across my skin with his every tongue lash.

When I thought I could no longer stand the intense tension coursing through my entire body and the throbbing heat growing deep inside my empty vagina, Chad's magical mouth seared over my pussy in one hot fusion.

I exploded!

I cried out Chad's name as the spasms ripped through me in a tsunami of pleasure.

Stretch grabbed my chin and turned my head and then his warm lips melted over mine, cutting off my cries. He kissed me hard and I kept convulsing within the hot shudders that were ripping me apart.

Instinctively I gyrated my hips and fought against Chad's hands on my inner thighs as he held me apart so he could mouth fuck me into oblivion.

He sucked hard and then he slipped his tongue into me, thrusting like a little cock and then withdrawing, licking, and lapping until I was panting and bucking, convulsing with every pleasure hit.

And then Stretch ripped his mouth away at the same time Chad's lips left my body. I felt Stretch moving me until I was entirely upon his body.

I could barely register what was going on as I kept bucking and writhing. The spasms were controlling me and I could barely keep my eyes open as I watched Chad rise up.

In a quick move, he reached out and grabbed a condom from Stretch who was huffing and puffing beneath me. His every breath made his cock tremble in my ass, creating even more spasms. My body flared with heat and I loved it.

In seconds, Chad sheathed himself and then he was moving his muscular body over me.

He lowered himself and I cried out as his mouth melted over mine, then his hard chest flattened my breasts and his thick, juicy penis plunged into my spasming vagina in one solid thrust.

With two cocks buried inside me, I exploded even harder!

Chad withdrew and thrust into me again.

His strokes were persistent and never ending as my vaginal muscles clamped around him and tried to hold him inside. But he was stronger, his cock driving pleasure throughout my entire body.

The sounds of male groans intermingled with my cries of arousal. Shudders raged through me. It was never ending and I loved it!

As the insane spasms began to ebb, Stretch's body tightened and he convulsed beneath me as he orgasmed. Soon after, Chad joined him.

Afterwards, I fell asleep between the two men. Their body heat was so welcome and I much preferred this heat to that horrific icy cold that my two lifeguards had thankfully chased out of me.

Yes, I owed both of them my life and their gratitude for giving me a new outlook on sex.

Sometime during the night, the storm ceased and when morning dawned, I discovered that Chad had rolled off me. I gazed around and found him standing at the lone window of the first aid shack.

Slowly, I managed to untangle myself from Stretch. His cock was still buried inside my ass and he was fast asleep and snoring softly. He seemed oblivious when I managed to climb off him, his cock leaving me with a succulent pop.

I was pleasantly tender in both openings from the sex, but I knew I could get used to this kind of soreness.

I joined Chad at the window and I was surprised when he reached out and slipped his arm around my waist, pulling me up against his hard, muscular body.

"I'd kiss you good morning, Katie, but I've got morning breath," he whispered. A sweet smile brightened his face.

I grinned and he nodded out the window.

"The landline is working. I've already called for assistance. In the meantime, take a look at what you've been missing all these years without seeing a bunch of sunrises."

My breath caught as I gazed out.

Warm hues of purple, bright orange and baby blue colors splashed across the sky and reflected in the quiet glass-like ocean.

"It's so beautiful," I whispered.

Chad hugged me closer.

"So are you."

"Oh, wow. Such a nice compliment. Thank you," I replied.

My body was humming at his words and I wondered how he would respond with what I was about to ask him.

"I had a spectacular night with the two of you. Would you be up for doing it again?"

I held my breath and studied his face as I waited for his answer. He looked serious and was biting his bottom lip.

Such an endearing gesture.

"Katie, I would be willing to do anything to please you. From here on out, would you be my girl again?"

"As long as I am your *only* girl," I replied honestly.

I hoped my jealousy wouldn't ruin it this time around, but I would set boundaries so he knew I wanted to be his one and only.

"And I will be available to you in the sexual department any time you want. I'll continue coming here every day to swim but not to train for the Olympics anymore and when you get the urge to share, I want to be that woman in the manwich. Deal?"

Chad nodded.

"As I said earlier, Katie. I will do anything to please you and if that means you want to be sexually adventurous then I am all in. Deal."

His brown eyes glittered with happiness and I suddenly realized that Chad *was* the man with future written all over him. *The* man for me.

I couldn't have asked for a better guy.

The End

Taken by Three Bodyguards

Twenty-one-year-old Stephanie Stephenson has been in a safehouse with her three sexy bodyguards for many months. She's a lone witness to a murder and they've been protecting her from Santonio, the mob boss, who has vowed revenge if she dared to testify. It's all been strictly professional and platonic with her hunky bodyguards. Now the trial is over and Stephanie is free to go.

But her three bodyguards have other plans for Stephanie...very naughty plans.

Copyright

Taken by Three Bodyguards
By Jasmine Black
Published by Spunky Girl Publishing
Copyright December 2022 Jasmine Black
Cover Design by Talina Perkins ~ Bookin' It Designs

Author Note

This is a work of fiction. Characters, places, settings, and events presented in this book are purely of the author's imagination and bear no resemblance to any actual person, living or dead or to any actual events, places, and/or settings.

Chapter One

"It's a nice view," Kenneth stated as he stepped onto the front porch behind me.

I inhaled as his succulent body heat curled around me. The man made me shiver, but in a really good way.

The wine glass in my hand trembled as I gazed out across the meadow of the New Hampshire countryside safe house, which was a white clapboard farmhouse that had been repossessed during the Great Recession of two thousand and eight and then sold to the security firm that the prosecutor's office had hired to protect me.

It was a nice view just like Kenneth said. The tall green meadow grass swayed in the hot July breeze and in the distance, a misty purple haze danced upon the blue ocean. So peaceful. So quiet. I'd enjoyed this view during the seasons while staying here. I'd miss it.

I'd been the main witness against the mob boss, Santonio, who'd killed my co-worker, right in front of me.

Jayne, a new waitress like myself, had worked at this ritzy downtown New York Italian restaurant. We'd been on the evening shift serving a lone gentleman in a private back dining room. She'd been shot in the head at close range for daring to say no to an invitation for her to sit down and have dinner with him. I'd been the only witness.

I'd been lucky to escape with my life, getting a mere bullet wound to my shoulder as I'd run screaming out of the room. I'd had no idea that mafia members frequented the five-star restaurant. Or that

Santonio had a very bad temper and had just found out his wife was having an affair with a competing mob boss.

Good thing for me, Santonio had been a bad shot with a moving target.

The prosecution had managed to press charges in record time and Santonio's criminal defence lawyers hadn't been able to come up with any excuses to protect their client. They'd tried to trash my reputation, but I was a good girl, an only child, with a solid mom and dad. The trial had been speedy.

An earlier phone call we'd received today from a reporter friend of my bodyguards, had let us know that the mob boss had been found guilty. He wouldn't be getting out of prison any time soon and it was such a relief for me. Now that the trial was finally over and he was behind bars, this would be my last day here.

Until today, the bodyguards had been almost perfect gentlemen, but along the way there had been signs of their interest in me. Due to my trauma at getting shot and witnessing Jayne's death, I'd been able to ignore those signs. But now that I was free, I realized my three bodyguards wanted more than to protect me.

Instincts told me that they *wanted* me.

But that wasn't going to happen, even if they did make my pussy purr and whipped a fevered heat through me whenever they looked at me. I just wanted to put everything behind me, and I couldn't do that with any one of them in my life. No matter how hot and sexy they might be and I certainly didn't want them to know how limited my sexual experience was either.

I was practically a virgin at the age of twenty-one, having had one brief sexual intercourse episode in my late teens with a neighbor boy. The condom had broken right in the middle of him orgasming. I'd been terrified of getting pregnant and reality had crashed in around me that the guy wouldn't stand by me if he'd knocked me up.

He would have had the pleasure of screwing me and I would have got stuck with a baby. Once my period had come, I'd vowed never to take that kind of chance again. I would wait and have sex when I was married or at the very least start having sex when I could support myself and a baby.

So far, I'd kept that promise to myself.

After that phone call from the reporter, I had immediately noticed the news had changed the mood with my three bodyguards. Suddenly it didn't appear to be business as usual.

Celebrating over a bottle of red wine, I had been confronted with their sultry looks and an unusual silence. Even my usual friendly, flirty banter hadn't loosened things up.

So, I gave up. I mean, I wasn't responsible for their dour moods, right? So, I'd stepped outside to look at the lovely view one final time.

"We've been here how long?" Kenneth asked after a lengthy silence.

"Ten months, two weeks, three days and four hours," I answered, without looking at him.

"She's been counting the days?" Joshua laughed from behind the porch screen door, a mere few feet away from me. There was something strange in his laugh. Something off. I just didn't know what.

I tensed as I hadn't known he was there. But his laughter was a good sign, wasn't it?

"Yeah, it seems like she can't wait to get out of here, and away from us," Edward chimed in.

He had been listening as well.

"Is that true? You don't like our company?" Kenneth asked.

His voice sounded deep and daring. Like he was still upset.

Kenneth was the tallest of my bodyguards and they were all well over six-feet compared to my five-foot five plump figure. As he gazed down at me with his dark green eyes and a frown on his face, I felt like a trapped she-cat with three tom cats stalking her.

I shivered at their remarks. I could feel the sexual tension zipping through the air and my body betraying me.

My breasts were suddenly feeling heavy as I craved their hands touching me there and to my annoyance, a hot wetness seeped down my quivering vagina as I imagined Kenneth sliding his cock into me right here on the porch.

I blew out a tense breath. I had hoped to avoid an awkward goodbye. But it appeared that wasn't going to happen.

I gulped down the rest of my wine, trying to gather courage. It was unprofessional, wasn't it, for them, and for me, to be dallying with the idea of having sex?

And who would I have sex with? Joshua, Edward? Or Kenneth?

I just couldn't pick. They were all hot looking, well muscled men. I had enjoyed all their company, but the risk of sex and getting pregnant rolled like an ominous warning at the back of my head.

I sighed. didn't dare offend them more than I already apparently had, so I'd best just high tail it out of here before I caved into my naughty cravings to taste test one of them. Or all of them.

My cheeks suddenly went hot.

No, not possible. I was just fantasizing about a menage. Stuff like that just happened in books.

I shook those crazy thoughts of having sex with them away.

Despite my seeing glimpses of their hot stares over the months, the impressive erections tenting their pants when they thought I hadn't been paying attention, they'd made me feel safe.

That is, until today.

Until now.

I tensed as the screen door creaked open behind me. Joshua and Edward had joined Kenneth.

I gathered up my courage and turned to face them. My breath backed up at their dark, sensual looks as they stared down at me.

Chapter Two

I swallowed, wishing my wine glass were once again full, instead of empty. I set the glass upon the porch railing. I had the feeling I should run. Escape these three bodyguards who, until today, I had trusted implicitly.

I tried to keep the trembling that I was feeling out of my voice, but it came through loud and clear for all three to hear.

"Sure, I've enjoyed your company. Now I must go on with my life and you guys have to go on with your next assignment, right? I thank you very much for all your help. I owe you big time."

Edward chuckled and stepped closer to me. His dark brown eyes twinkled, despite the sultry expression and I don't know what made me look down, but I did and I noticed a large bulge pressing against his pants.

My breath stalled in my throat. He was turned on big time. I resisted the urge to check out the other two guys.

"Oh baby, you more than owe us. You've been teasing us all this time. And we've held back," Edward said.

"Yeah, Stephanie. You are the worst tease. And now that the job is over, we don't have to be professional anymore, now do we?" Joshua added.

Oh boy. I had no idea I had been teasing them. I'd just been my friendly, flirty self. I had meant them no harm. Sure, I'd had naughty flares of desire for each of the guys, but I'd never intended on acting on it.

"Well, yes, you do need to be professional. I've got to pack and someone needs to drive me to the airport so I can meet up with my boyfriend." I had lied. There was no boyfriend.

"Oh? Really? You sure have been keeping this guy a secret," Kenneth said in a cool voice.

"Yeah, who is this guy? He must be pretty solid by now, waiting for you all this time," Edward chuckled, one dark eyebrow arched in a questioning manner.

"Just as solid as we are, right babe?" Joshua whispered.

I tensed as Edward reached out. He brushed my arm as he grabbed the empty wine glass and to my surprise disappointment shot through me. I had thought maybe something naughty was going to happen. But yeah, best if it didn't.

"Well, I'll catch up with you all in a bit. Just going to pack. Bye for now," I said with a wave and headed back inside the house.

Whew. I hadn't even realized how excited I'd gotten with all three men standing so close to me, their eyes all dark and sensual like that.

Yeah, I'd best get packed before something bad happened. I hurried into my bedroom.

It took me longer than I'd thought to get everything together. After getting shot, and getting out of the hospital, I hadn't been allowed to go back to my apartment. Even my parents hadn't been allowed to contact me. They'd stuck me in witness protection and I'd had to buy all new clothes and personal items.

As I opened the last drawer, my mouth dropped open and shock zipped over me. I quickly realized these were items I had not purchased. A large dildo, vibrators, nipple clamps and there were other toys that I couldn't see, due to the discreet packaging.

My tummy hollowed out in a nervous feeling. What in the world was going on? Embarrassment rushed through me. If I thought my cheeks were hot earlier, they were on fire now.

"Your going away presents," Kenneth's voice startled me.

I turned from the toys and found him casually leaning against the doorway. His arms were crossed and he was watching me with his green eyes. Predatory eyes that told me his interest in me had now come fully to the surface and he wasn't going to hide it anymore.

He had changed his clothes too. Earlier he'd worn the traditional army fatigues that I had seen them in almost all the time. Now he wore black slacks and a white silk shirt. He looked nice in regular clothing, not that he didn't look great in his camouflage attire, but yeah, he looked...approachable now.

"I'm sure my boyfriend will be asking what those toys are all about," I said, completely surprised that I had been able to come up with such a remark so quickly when my body was flaming with excitement and nervousness.

He straightened. For a second, I thought he was going to leave but then he walked into my bedroom with a confident stroll that had my breath backing up in my lungs. I struggled to steady my hands as I closed the drawer.

"You're not taking them with you? I'm sure your boyfriend will enjoy using them on you. I'm sure you'll enjoy them too," he said in a sultry tone. He stopped a couple of feet away from me. He was so close I could smell his sexy aftershave and a hint of soap.

"We can buy toys ourselves," I replied.

I lifted one of my packed suitcases from my bed and placed it on the floor between the two of us. Kind of like a barrier.

He was studying me. His green eyes seemed darker now, full of intent. Despite my uneasiness, the way he was observing me had something naughty brewing deep inside my pussy and my skin felt sensitive, needy for his touches.

A fine sheen of perspiration blossomed across my forehead and I suddenly felt the need to get away from him because I knew everything I'd worked for in keeping a man out of my bed, just might be undone here.

"You don't have a boyfriend, do you, Stephanie? You don't have a lover. Maybe you've never had a man..." he whispered.

He was slowly shaking his head like he was disappointed and damned if I couldn't stop myself from doing the same.

"I didn't think so."

I could barely hear him; his voice was so low. But I could hear the sexiness there in his tone. The raw need. The animalistic self-control that could unravel in an instant.

"Maybe, I want to be your lover," he said.

"I...I...that's not possible," I replied.

I couldn't think with him being so near to me. Couldn't even inhale. I felt heady at his admission. Unwanted excitement ripped through me.

"Why not, sweetums?" he pressed. *Sweetums*, their nickname for me. I have a bit of a bulging belly from eating too many sweets. For some reason, they liked that about me.

"It's none of your business, Kenneth." I didn't want him find out about how truly inexperienced I was.

"What would you say if I told you I wanted to make it my business?"

"It wouldn't work. I need to go." I picked up the suitcase.

"I want to make love to you, Stephanie."

His boldness made me drop the suitcase. I felt weak in my knees. I couldn't believe what I was hearing.

"Excuse me? This really is unprofessional, Ken."

"I'm off the clock now. The gig is over. Nothing unprofessional about it. I want you. I want to lay you naked on that bed. I want to kiss every part of you. Make love to every inch of you."

I didn't know what to say. My thoughts were whirling. His stare was telling me he was the kind of man who got what he wanted and he wanted me.

"We've heard you masturbate in your bedroom at nights," he said softly.

Wow, and here I'd thought I'd kept quiet when I'd fantasized about them. I felt so hot now from embarrassment, I thought I would self combust.

"We know you must be needing some release after all this time without a man."

"We?" I managed to say, catching that word.

"We all want to be inside of you, Stephanie. All of us plunging into you at the same time. Your mouth, your pussy, your ass."

Oh, dear heavens. What was I going to do?

Chapter Three

I trembled at the thought of having three men thrusting into me. I could never allow something like that. I wasn't *that* kind of girl.

"We want to bring you so much pleasure that you'll never go back to masturbating. We'll ruin you, Steph. Ruin you, for good."

I could only stand there, shocked by what he was saying. He bent down and picked up my suitcase and leisurely placed it off to the side. Then he casually picked up the other packed suitcases on my bed and placed them beside the wall, out of the way.

I had a few moments for a chance to escape while he was pre-occupied. But did I want to escape? He was offering me something I'd only fantasized about.

But they were all big, tall men. How *big* would their cocks be? I felt myself creaming. Felt my defiance weakening.

Kenneth turned to me, a rabid hunger in his gaze. Any escape was gone. Doubts of having sex with him were disappearing fast as he stepped closer and towered over me.

I felt hot as he stared down at me. Wicked lust flared in his green eyes.

"You just enjoy and we'll do all that needs doing," he said.

The tip of his pink tongue peeked out from between his lips and I noticed the gold ball piercing there right in the middle of his tongue. I'd fantasized about that tongue. About how that miniature gold ball would feel on my body.

I tensed as he reached up. His long fingers unbuttoned my blouse and then he gently opened the sides, revealing my pink bra to him.

"Pretty in pink," he commented as he slid my blouse over my shoulders.

I blew out a breath as he tossed my garment onto a nearby dresser. Then he reached for the bra straps and lowered them over my arms.

Oh, have mercy. No man, except my doctor or that neighbourhood guy, had seen my intimate areas.

My breasts spilled free from their cups, and he let out a low whistle. Appreciation flared in his gaze.

"Sexy, just as I knew they would be," Kenneth commented.

I gasped as he reached out with both his hands and then gently brushed my nipples with his thumbs. My buds immediately puckered and hardened and an exquisite need for a harder rubbing pulsed through me.

Hot liquid gushed down my vagina. My pussy felt swollen, heavy.

"You like that, don't you sweetums?" he cooed.

I could barely nod.

"I knew you would."

"I don't...don't want to get pregnant," I blurted. That was my worst fear. Getting pregnant, especially now that I was unemployed. It was best that my fear was out in the open and then maybe I could just simply submit to my naughty side.

He shook his head.

"You'll get pregnant only when we want you to."

Only when we want you too. Okay, that was a weird reply.

But I couldn't form a question as to what he meant because my thoughts were whirling as he cupped my breasts and lowered his head.

He sucked my right nipple into his mouth and I moaned at the sultry pressure of a man's hot lips on my sensitive flesh. Immediately I felt the gold round metal on his tongue circling my nipple, then pressing against it. Wicked sensations burned through me.

Automatically I reached out and cupped the back of his neck. My vagina quivered as I imagined his mouth *down* there between my thighs.

He licked and lapped at my nipple with his bristly tongue, then he scraped his teeth over my sensitive bud creating an exhilarating lightning pain. A forceful sucking followed, which unleashed a powerful surge of excitement that speared spasms into my clitoris and vagina. Even my ass was clenching!

I moaned and instinctively gyrated my hips, needing more.

This was crazy. Wonderfully crazy.

My breathing was so out of control and my hands were at his neck pulling him closer into my breast. But he was like solid stone. His head never wavered. The pressure of his tongue never increased or decreased. He was in full control and the need to have him sinking his cock into my tightening vagina was pounding through me like a tornado.

I was gasping and keening and then he moved over to my other breast. His hands were massaging my flesh as he took my other nipple into his mouth. His tongue swirled and lapped. The small metal ball smoothed and circled my nipple and then his teeth nipped until I was crying out from the pain. Then he soothed the hurt with forceful sucks that created such sweet pleasure, I could barely stand it.

By the time he was finished, I was on my tippy toes and gasping. He drew back his head, allowing me to see my nipples. They were red, swollen like cherries and oh, so achy.

What had he done to me? My nipples were on fire. I was on fire.

Suddenly I heard a noise from behind Kenneth. I peeked around his shoulder and embarrassment and awe unleashed through me.

Standing just inside the bedroom door were Joshua and Edward. They were watching us.

And they were both naked!

My knees went weak as awareness brought on a whole new meaning of maybe I can have sex with these men. Especially since they really *wanted* me.

Their bodies looked hard and fit. Muscles rippled everywhere, and I mean everywhere, as they stroked their long, thick erections. Their gazes were fixed on me and I trembled at their lusty expressions.

Kenneth stepped to the side, giving them a close-up view of me, without my blouse and bra on. I resisted the urge to cover my breasts, to hide my tender, hard and very plump nipples that poked out at them from Kenneth's sucking. I suddenly wanted to act mature, like this wasn't embarrassing me. So I kept my arms to my sides.

"She's a beauty, just like you said she'd be," Joshua said.

"Yeah, well worth the wait," Edward added.

I found it hard to breathe as both men continued to watch me and stroke their perfectly huge cocks. Hard, purplish flesh with mushroom shaped cockheads, angling stiffly and swollen, upward toward their taut abdomens. Big cocks that demanded action. Needed release.

My goodness! I'd been staying here in this safe house with these perfect specimens of men and had only thought of them as my saviours, protecting me from the evil Santonio, who'd vowed revenge if I dared testify against him.

Wow, this could not be a better reward for all my nighttime fantasies and my what I had thought was quiet masturbating.

"Why don't you let me take over, Ken. Get yourself ready," Edward said as he stepped toward me.

Kenneth made some sort of grunt and I heard the rustle of clothing. But I didn't dare look at him. All I could do was focus on Edward as he stepped in front of me, with his engorged shaft.

He's not wearing protection, my mind warned.

Chapter Four

B ut I was already lost within my body trembles and anticipation of things to come as Edward cupped my breasts and began pinching my achy nipples. I closed my eyes as he lowered his head and kissed me. His mouth was hard, possessive as his lips sipped and sucked and then lightning zipped through my mouth as his tongue stroked into me. Hard and fast, he dueled with my meek tongue, until I responded to his challenging mouth and kissed him back, my hands grabbing around his waist as I tried to pull him toward me.

I wanted to feel his shaft sink into me. Wanted him to fuck me, but he was like a solid pillar of stone. Unmoveable, just like Kenneth had been.

Man! What was it with these guys? So rigid. So in control.

Edward kissed me harder, until I saw an array of brilliant stars. Silver, gold, red.

By the time he was finished with me, I felt as if I was just nipples and a mouth.

He drew his head away and his gaze was dark and determined.

"Remove the rest of your clothes," Edward instructed.

Something hot and heavy pooled in my lower belly. My thighs felt tight. My pussy wet.

Now that I had a moment to gather my thoughts, I was hesitant. Was this really happening? It was happening so fast.

"Come on, baby. Let's see the rest of you. I know it'll be just as pretty," Kenneth coaxed from nearby.

I glanced his way and my breath caught. He was now fully naked and stroking his big shaft.

I was really going to go through with this?

I blew out a tense breath and reached down. They were watching my every move and suddenly exhilaration soared through me that three men would be so turned on by me.

But I wasn't used to this. Having men watching me undress, was something unusual and heat flushed into my cheeks.

I swallowed and kicked off my running shoes and unzipped my jeans. I lowered them. Stepped out of them. I stood in front of my three bodyguards with only my panties on.

They looked approvingly at me and I felt so hot that I could barely stand it. Perspiration blossomed across my forehead.

"Go on," Joshua whispered.

I did as he said, slipped my fingers under the waistband of my panties and slid them down, then let them puddle at my ankles, before stepping out of them.

"Very nice," Edward said. "So tell us, sweetums. How did you fantasize about us while you masturbated?"

Oh my!

"Did you imagine we would do this to you?" Joshua asked as he stepped behind me.

I made a move to look back, but Edward grabbed my elbow.

"Don't look at him, baby. I want your full attention on me. Now bend over at your waist, and hold onto my hips, nice and tight," he instructed.

He was pulling my elbow downward as he spoke. I really didn't resist. With three very strong men surrounding me, how could I? Not that I wanted to. I wanted more of what Kenneth and Joshua had already given me.

I did as Edward asked and quickly realized what he wanted me to do, especially now that his cock was mere inches from my mouth.

"Have you ever done oral on a man before?" Edward asked.

I shook my head and shivered at the sight of his erect penis.

"Good. A virgin," his voice was hoarse and dark.

I yelped as hands slid against my inner thighs.

"We want you nice and wide. Spread wider. Kenneth, get me that lube," came Joshua's growl.

Lube. Oh, my goodness.

"Here," came Kenneth's reply. I heard the smack of a lube tube being slapped into Joshua's hand.

I did what Joshua said, widening my stance and moaned as Edward's palms slid up and down my inner thighs. I felt them tighten and quiver at his touches. Then his hands caressed the curves of my ass cheeks. Nice and slow. A moment later, his fingers dipped between my crack and began to gently massage me there.

"Now open your mouth, baby. Time for some delicacy. No biting. Just explore. Lick and lap and suck. Got it?"

I nodded. My heart thundered in my ears as he moved his cock closer.

I opened my mouth.

I hesitated and looked up at Edward. His gaze was tortured and savage.

"Go on, baby. Suck it," he growled.

His cock looked angry at this close range. Enraged and big.

I shut my eyes as he pushed his fiery shaft against my lips, his mushroom shaped cockhead going in just barely an inch. Excitement and lust pounded through me as I licked underneath. His flesh was hot, solid and so velvety.

Edward moaned at my touch.

"Wrap your hands around the base of my shaft. Only let it go in as far as you can manage."

I nodded, encouraged by his words. I grabbed the base of his pulsing shaft and moved my head closer, allowing the rest of his cockhead to enter my mouth.

"Start sucking, sweet baby. Bob your head. Suck and bob. You can do that, can't you?"

He sounded impatient.

I could. I knew I could. I did as he asked and my lips tightened on his swollen penis.

Suddenly he grabbed the top of my hair and held on, evoking an erotic pain shooting through my scalp. Then he thrust his hips forward and his cock went deeper into my mouth, stretching my lips and then he withdrew and thrust in again.

Oh, okay. I think I got the idea. My mouth would be a vagina for him. Nice and tight. I slurped on his flesh and sucked and with my tongue caressed underneath.

"That's it. Keep going," he said in a tortured voice. The grip on my scalp tightened, the pain, erotic. He moved his hips faster in and out of my mouth while I bobbed my head trying to keep up to his pistoning.

"Good, nice and steady. Go ahead, Josh," Edward instructed.

Behind me, I could feel Joshua's hands stop caressing my ass. It had felt good, having his palms rubbing my cheeks, his fingers massaging my protesting sphincter.

"She's pretty tight, back here," Joshua said.

"Here, I've lubed a dildo, it'll loosen her up," Kenneth said from behind her.

"Hey, thanks," I heard Joshua say.

"Yeah, well I get first dibs after you take her," Kenneth replied.

I blinked at how casually they were talking about me, as if I wasn't even there.

"Keep sucking, sweetums. Don't let them distract you," Edward snapped.

I focused back to his jerking shaft. It had grown immensely in my mouth and it was bruising my lips.

I nodded my head, slurping his shaft. I was starting to love the silky strong feel of his pulsating flesh in my mouth. Starting to enjoy his guttural groans of appreciation and the sparks of pain in my scalp as he held tight to my hair and thrust his hips faster.

"Harder!" he suddenly shouted.

I sucked and tightened my mouth even more.

I jolted as suddenly my ass flamed with pain and heat as something slapped across my right ass cheek. Then more pain across my left ass cheek.

Oh my God! They were spanking me!

Chapter Five

Another slap! Ouch! And another. More pain, more heat. More slaps. Each hit had my face pushing into Edward, whom it appeared, was lost in his pleasure as he bucked into my mouth in a frantic pace.

I exhaled a tense breath but forced myself to keep sucking as Edward's penis was jerking and pulsing and then hot jets of his release flooded my mouth. I quickly gulped and swallowed, enjoying the warm liquid going down my parched throat.

His body shook and lurched and I opened my eyes to look upward to see the exquisite desire splashing across his features. His eyes were scrunched tight and his lips were parted as he panted.

Wow, I gave this guy such pleasure just with my mouth. It was amazing.

When his shaft went limp, he withdrew and opened his eyes. He stared down at me, but kept his hand tangled in my hair. His face was serene and satisfied but there was an odd flare in his expression. Was it pity? Sorrow?

Before I could even fathom as to why he was looking at me like that, I felt my ass cheeks being pulled apart and something round, big and wet pressed against my sphincter. I gasped at the intensity of the pressure.

"Just relax and keep the position and keep holding onto Edward. Inhale and exhale, nice and slow. I'm going to prepare you. This dildo is just a little smaller than we are and nicely lubed," Joshua whispered.

I flinched as a hand touched my right very hot ass cheek, but it was a caress this time.

Soft and gentle.

I relaxed and wondered what they had in store for me next.

"This will hurt so good because you aren't used to it...yet. So, just relax and accept," Joshua said.

Easier said than done and why had he just said, you aren't used to it, yet? Do they think I am staying?

I whimpered as the pressure increased and then my muscles gave way and the dildo slid into me.

"Yeah, nice and tight," Joshua murmured.

"The tighter the better," Edward commented from above me.

I flushed at their remarks. My cheeks were now just as hot as my flaming ass.

Joshua pushed the dildo deeper and deeper. The pressure was incredible and I was feeling sore now.

He slid out the toy. I heard slurps of lube and then the item was pressing into me again. This time even deeper. My goodness! I was being stretched so impossibly. Then he slowly withdrew and began a gentle pistoning motion that I liked. It was soothing. In and out. In and out.

I realized my ass was now clenching the lubed toy and my pussy was feeling hot and neglected.

"You look beautiful, sweetums. I can tell you like it by the way your face is all scrunched," Edward commented from above me.

I nodded jerkily. Suddenly wanting to please them was everything to me. To see them happy would be ideal.

I kept my eyes closed and enjoyed Joshua's grunts and the rhythmic thrusting. I could feel how his powerful shaft moved inside of me. Could feel every inch pressing against my anal muscles and how lovingly my anus gripped his solid flesh in welcome.

Then Joshua began thrusting faster, harder and I found myself imagining him pistoning his cock into me. Automatically my hips began to sway and I held tighter to Edward.

"She's enjoying it. Very good," Kenneth said from somewhere behind me.

His approval thrilled me. Why in the world had I even thought about running from this exquisite excitement? These three men had protected me. Had put their lives on the line for me. They deserved a little going away present from me. I deserved some hot and heavy sex too, especially if they were interested in giving it so freely.

"Let's see if she likes the real thing," Joshua said. His voice was hoarse now as he pulled the toy out of me. My heart began a fast beat as I heard the slurp of lube.

Fear suddenly twisted through me. Hadn't he said the dildo wasn't as big as him? And his cock was big.

"Don't tense up on us now," I heard Edward say with a chuckle.

I opened my eyes and gazed up at him. His look was gentle and my heart twisted at even being frightened. I forced myself to relax.

I quaked as Joshua's lubed mushroom-shaped cockhead pushed against my tight ring of muscles. Whimpered as he thrust into me, hard and fast. Pleasure pain burst through my ass and I dug my fingers into Edward's waist, suddenly noticing his cock was starting to become erect again right before my eyes.

Have mercy! He was getting turned on seeing me like this. He must have a stimulating view, looking down and watching my ass getting impaled by a man while I held onto him for dear life.

Joshua's cock was ultra-thick and my anal muscles protested his heavy invasion. Pinpricks of pain was soothed by sharp pleasure as he began a slow thrust. Every thrust deeper than the last one.

"She's taking it like a pro!" I heard Kenneth comment.

I moaned with every impalement. Keened with ever withdrawal.

Then Joshua was pistoning. Hard and fast and I gyrated my hips, loving the velvety length of his pole burying itself inside of me. The bites of pain were erotic and I craved more of it.

"Look what you've been missing, baby," Joshua ground out. He withdrew and he began slapping my ass again. Fiery pain and heat blossomed across my bottom as the palms of his hands smacked my sensitive flesh. I could only imagine how red my cheeks must look.

"Yeah, that's nice. A blushing ass always turns me on," he growled.

I yelped as he spanked me harder and harder. The heat spread through me like a fire, consuming me and then he was thrusting his cock into me again. Quicker, more forceful.

To my surprise, I felt the stirrings of an orgasm. How was this possible? Just from anal? My vagina tightened; my thighs quivered. My pussy dropped and felt so heavy and swollen. I ached to have it touched. To have it impaled like my ass.

Joshua's breathing grew rougher and then suddenly he was climaxing. Warm liquid gushed deep within, his cock jerked and swelled and he bucked harder and then he groaned and shouted.

Pleasure began to build within my lower belly. I could feel the spasms of a climax forming. It was nearing. I could feel it!

Then he was pulling out and disappointment rocked me.

No, don't stop! Please!

I don't know if I spoke aloud or if it was just in my head, but either way, I knew I wanted more. So much more!

"Let's tie her to the bed. She's a keeper," I heard Joshua mutter.

I licked my lips as nervousness pummelled me, but I was darkly excited as well. Had they already ruined me? Ruined me like Kenneth had warned me they would do?

"Why...why do you want to tie me to the bed?" I asked Edward as he helped me to stand. My legs felt weak and my ass felt open, wonderfully used. I wanted it filled again. I trembled at that thought.

"Oh, sweet baby, your inexperience is showing. It's turning me on so much," Kenneth said as he stood beside the bed, stroking his extremely swollen and erect shaft.

Chapter Six

Embarrassment lashed me. I hadn't wanted them to discover how innocent I truly was, but now I'd given myself away.

Edward led me to the bed and I spied ropes with cuffs tied to the headboard.

I swallowed and quivered.

"Don't you trust us?" Edward asked as he patted the mattress.

I nodded. I did trust them. And my ass was on fire and so were my nipples. I couldn't run away now. I needed them to put out the fire. I was shaken and my body was utterly full of desire. I felt weak, submissive.

I sat upon the bed and then lay down, loving the warmth of the soft blankets beneath me.

My three bodyguards stared down at me, their intent gazes raking over my naked body. The air seemed hot from their stares and I could feel the sexual tension zipping between me and them.

Three tall, very naked, very aroused men. Toned muscles. Tanned bodies. I especially couldn't take my eyes off the bulging length of their cocks. They were so thick, flushed and engorged with blood. And both Joshua and Edward were erect again!

"You like what you see, don't you, baby?" Edward asked as he lifted my arm up over my head and attached a cuff to my wrist.

"I...yes," I whispered.

"Good," Joshua said as he walked to the other side of the bed, his swollen shaft bobbing with his stride.

He restrained my other wrist.

"Now, let's see what awesome sweets you've got hidden between your legs, shall we? Spread, so we can get a good look," Kenneth said from the foot of the bed.

I creamed as I did as he asked. I held my breath when the mattress moved and he climbed onto the bed. He positioned his wide shoulders between my legs.

"Oh," I gasped and clenched my fists as his hands slipped beneath my flaming ass cheeks.

He lifted my bottom and then he dipped his head. I hissed as his hot breath whispered against my pussy. Cried out as he lapped his tongue over my quivering clitoris, his tongue like a hot brand as it licked and caressed and stroked.

My vagina clenched and I was suddenly awash in desperation as he continued his erotic assault. I could feel my cream gushing down my vagina, could hear him slurping it into his mouth.

He moaned; his tone appreciative.

I could feel his hot moist tongue spreading my labia, licking and nibbling at my sensitive folds. My breathing grew faster. My body grew tenser.

He circled my clit and then my anticipation grew as he drew closer and closer to my vagina again. Then he was licking at the opening. Sucking and slurping and teasing until I could feel the insane hunger for an orgasm powering through me.

As I concentrated on what he was doing to me, I was barely aware of the sounds of his lapping as it filled the bedroom. Then there was movement coming in from both sides of me. Joshua and Edward were now on the bed, their heads lowering, their hands cupping my breasts as their mouths zeroed in on my nipples.

I cried out as their hot lips sucked onto my ultra-tender nipples. I moaned as their teeth nibbled, causing red-hot pain and pleasure.

The area between my thighs was on fire as Kenneth continued lapping and licking and sucking. I twisted against the restraints, trying to escape the pleasure shivers. But there was no way out. Did I even want to escape? My thoughts were disintegrating as I was sucked into simply feeling what was happening to my body.

Heat flared through every part of me as their fiery mouths seduced my intimate parts. The sensations they created were intoxicating, addictive and I needed more. Automatically I lifted my legs and slammed my feet down upon Kenneth's back, digging my heels into his hard muscles, squeezing my thighs against his head for a deeper pressure.

Then suddenly Kenneth thrust his long tongue into my quivering vagina and the hot desperation rushing through me exploded, showering me with shudders and spasms unlike any I'd ever experienced while masturbating.

I lost control as eager mouths sucked my nipples and my pussy.

I bucked and cried out as pleasure waves rained and consumed me. I arched my hips, cried out as Kenneth withdrew and then once again he teasingly lapped at my clit. Then he pistoned into me again. His devilish tongue was like a mini whip, lashing and snapping against my engorged clitoris and then it was like a mini-cock thrusting and plunging into my spasming vagina.

The spasms of pleasure wouldn't stop. It was all consuming, seeping through every muscle and igniting every sensitive nerve.

I jerked against the restraints and screamed and shuddered as nerve endings snapped with pain and muscles twisted with pleasure.

Their mouths made love to me.

The pleasure was insane. It was beautiful.

And I wanted to be lost in this lusty storm forever.

All too soon, my climax began to ebb.

"I need to take her, now," Kenneth suddenly said and stopped pleasuring me with his mouth.

Oh no! Keep going! I want another orgasm!

I dug my feet deeper into his back, but that didn't keep him in place. He simply lifted himself and my feet slid off him.

I trembled and looked over Edward and Joshua's heads as they continued sucking on my aching nipples. Kenneth moved his lower body into place between my thighs. His arms were braced on either side of my waist. His dark gaze captured and held mine and then he was lowering his torso.

Kenneth watched my face as he thrust into me, hard and fast and I cried out as his swollen shaft impaled me stretching my vaginal muscles as I'd never been stretched before. Immediately I exploded into another orgasm. I closed my eyes and rode the intensity.

Quickly, he withdrew and then began a firm, driving rhythm that had me shaking and convulsing within the tremendous spasms created by the incredible length of his stroking cock. I bucked and trembled and gasped as convulsions kept coming, tearing through me, ripping me apart and destroying my innocence.

Chapter Seven

My pussy clamped around his rigid flesh, spasming around him, trying to keep him from leaving. But he withdrew all too fast, and then sunk into me again. I shuddered and keened as I kept coming apart.

And then his plunges grew faster, frantic and beautifully brutal. I sensed he was nearing his climax. Suddenly he shouted out my name and then he came and I felt his wet release spurting inside of me. His sperm burying deep, making a claim.

A baby.

All too soon the spasms ebbed and I was left gasping.

Then Kenneth withdrew and climbed off me and left the bedroom. Just like that. I was disappointed to say the least.

Bip. Bam. Thank you, ma'am.

"I need to take her next." I heard Joshua's hoarse voice as both he and Edward stopped sucking on my nipples and moved their mouths off my nipples.

Mercy! More pleasure was coming. I needed to brace myself for the possibility of pregnancy. For some strange reason, the idea of becoming pregnant didn't horrify me as it once did. How could anything bad come out of such beautiful pleasure?

I shuddered as I watched Joshua lay down beside me on the bed. From out of nowhere he produced a condom and sheathed it upon his jerking cock. A penetrating yearning to have his swollen flesh buried inside of me grabbed hold. Despite having had already two climaxes, I craved another one.

"Okay, onto your knees. I'll put you into position," Edward growled.

I scrambled to my knees, eager to please and he grabbed me by my waist with both his hands. With one powerful swoop he was lifting me over Joshua. A second later, I could feel Joshua's condom sheathed cock sliding into me. His length was amazing. His girth, incredibly swollen and hot. He gazed up at me with excitement flaring in his eyes.

Edward let go of me and then Joshua's hands replaced his on my waist. Then Joshua drew me down on top of him. The touch of his hot chest against my breasts was intoxicating and his mouth bruised over mine as he kissed me. Inside of me, his cock jerked, pulsed and lengthened even more!

I heard the slurp of lube and instantly realized what was going to happen next. Edward was going to take me anally.

My breaths quickened and I instinctively tensed as lubed fingers pressed against my tender sphincter.

"Easy," Edward soothed.

Joshua's kisses grew more forceful, dragging my attention to kissing him back.

Edward pressed and massaged the lube into me and before long I felt my tight anal muscles relaxing, accepting and welcoming the slurpy thrust of first one, then two and then three fingers.

"Let's get this show on the road," Edward murmured coarsely and then I heard the rip of plastic. Was he putting on a condom?

The bed moved as he climbed onto the mattress. I felt Edward's condom sheathed cockhead nudge against my anus. He pushed into me and a sharp bite of pain seared along my nerve endings. I cried into Joshua's mouth at the immediate discomfort.

"Shhh," I heard Edward say.

Joshua kissed me harder.

The stretching length of Edward's shaft burned into me and then my anal muscles gave way allowing for a deeper penetration.

Heavens! I had no idea I could accommodate two cocks inside of me at the same time!

I moaned as Edward withdrew and then thrust into me again.

Edward began a powerful pistoning into my ass. I slapped my hands upon Joshua's shoulders, loving the hard contours of his muscles. I was sandwiched between two very muscular men and with the forceful impact of Edward's body slamming against mine, he pushed me into Joshua, which in turn plunged Joshua's cock deeper and deeper into me with each thrust.

Friction against my clitoris quickly lit the flames that blew through me like a wildfire.

In seconds, I was awash in arousal.

I shattered, screaming into Joshua's mouth as the two cocks jerked and moved inside of me like two writhing serpents. Pleasure raced through me, sinking bone-deep turning my muscles into a shuddering mess. Turning me into a quivering electrified ragdoll.

I drowned in the crashing waves. Rolled within the sensations after sensations, the hunger of it splitting me apart. Soon, I could feel Edward and Joshua tensing and then convulsing within their own release.

The shards of pleasure seemed endless, yet all too soon the magnificent spasms ebbed away and before long Edward was withdrawing and then pulling me off Joshua.

"Man! That was awesome!" Joshua growled as he joined Edward. Both were quickly leaving the bedroom. They deposited their condoms in a waste basket on the way out.

My naked body was trembling. My pussy and ass were throbbing and my nipples felt wonderfully used. I pulled a blanket over myself, trying to deal with what had just happened. Was I pregnant? Why didn't I care? Why did I want more sex with them even after the hasty way they'd left?

"So, was it as good as your fantasies?" Kenneth chuckled as he strolled into the bedroom. He held a bottle of red wine in one hand and a large goblet full of wine in his other hand. He appeared cheerful, with a bright smile on his face.

Okay, that was a good thing, wasn't it? The sex must have pleased him as it had certainly pleased me.

He wore black underwear but I could clearly make out the thick outline of his big shaft pressing against the cloth. He plopped himself down upon the mattress beside me and handed me the goblet of wine. Eagerly, I accepted the glass and didn't realize the blankets had lowered and my breasts were now exposed.

Chapter Eight

H is gaze immediately focused there. I didn't bother covering myself. Let him look.

"Better than any fantasies I could come up with," I whispered.

"Sorry, for leaving the way I did. But I just wanted to check on a noise I'd heard."

"Oh, that's okay."

It made me feel better knowing he hadn't left so abruptly because of me.

I was dying of thirst and drank the wine like it was water. The sweet liquid splashed against my tastebuds and soothed my parched throat.

"More?" he asked as he lifted the bottle.

"Yes," I answered.

"Good."

I held out the empty goblet and he poured me another drink.

I drank it just as fast and quickly as the first one. The buzz from the alcohol soon followed. It felt nice. I relaxed and resisted the urge to pull the blankets off my lower half so he could see how wet I was getting just looking at him.

Man, how quickly my attitude had changed. Earlier, I hadn't wanted to leave, now all I wanted was to have my three bodyguards making love to me all day and all night.

"Have another," he said easily and poured another glass.

"If I didn't know better, I'd think you were trying to get me drunk," I said with a laugh.

He chuckled, but it didn't quite reach his eyes.

Oh. Oh. Something was up. A sliver of alarm rippled through me.

"What?" I asked as I sipped.

"There's something I need to tell you," he said coolly.

"I realize you didn't use a condom. That I might get pregnant..."

"No, you won't get pregnant. We put birth control pills in your food over the last little while. So that's not the issue."

They had what? I couldn't believe what I was hearing.

Anger zipped through me.

How dare they put birth control pills into my food without my permission!

What is the issue?" I snapped. So, they'd been planning this seduction for some time.

Bastards.

He was looking at me kind of funny and I didn't like that look. Maybe they didn't want to keep me around? Maybe he hadn't had such a good time as I had had?

"Why don't you let me tell her." I jumped as a woman's voice echoed from behind Kenneth.

She stood in the doorway. She looked familiar. I'd seen her somewhere and then a cold wave of terror hit me. I remembered her from the trial.

"Mrs. Santonio," I whispered.

My gaze flew to Kenneth who looked sheepish.

"What's going on? Why is she here?"

Oh my God! Was Santonio's two-timing wife going to kill me? Was she here to finish the job that her husband hadn't been able to do?

I forced myself to remain calm, but my brain was trying to figure out how to get out of here alive and in one hell of a hurry.

"Don't look so worried," Mrs. Santonio laughed as she stepped into the room.

I'd only seen her before from across the courtroom. She was a beautiful woman and she reminded me of Lana Turner, a stunning blonde movie star, who starred in the classic movies I sometimes watched with my mom on the Net.

"I'm not going to kill you, if that's what has you looking so spooked," she purred.

To my surprise, she took the bottle from Kenneth and poured more wine into my goblet.

"The thought did cross my mind," I admitted. Could I trust that she was telling the truth? I searched her hands for a gun or a knife. She had none.

Gosh, up close she looked so perfect. Her straight shoulder length blonde hair didn't have a strand out of place and her face was immaculately done with makeup. I also noted that she had the prettiest blue eyes and longest black eyelashes I'd ever seen.

"I can see your bodyguards have been giving you a good time. Good, that's what we want."

I blinked. What was she saying?

"My dear husband has extended his hit on you. You're going to need to stay here indefinitely. We don't want our star witness to get killed, now do we. Especially now that he's appealing his sentence. If something happens to you, why then there wouldn't be a new trial and I want him in prison and out of my way, so I've hired your three bodyguards to keep you...shall we say...satisfied for the foreseeable future. No worries on your parents, they've been told and whole heartedly agree."

Huh? Had I just heard right? I had to stay here.

I wasn't sure if I should be disappointed that it appeared the men were getting paid to have sex with me, or if I should be thrilled that I was going to be in this pleasurable situation for who knew how long.

I decided on the latter. I was beyond thrilled.

"I trust they've done a good job up until now?" she asked. There was a knowing smile at the tips of her perfectly shaped red lips.

I nodded. My face grew hot. I realized that she was the noise that Kenneth had heard earlier.

"Good, then I'll send in the other two men and the four of you can have some more...exercise."

She placed the half-full bottle of wine onto the night table and left.

"Wow, this is quite the news. Another hit on me," I said.

Kenneth shrugged his bare shoulders and my insides jumped like a live wire as his muscles flexed everywhere.

"You know we'll protect you with our lives. You'll be safe," he said.

Then he took the wine goblet out of my hand and placed it beside the wine bottle.

"Hey, baby. There's plenty of time to celebrate later," he whispered.

There was an odd sound at the doorway and I spied Joshua and Edward standing there. They were both naked, stroking their fully erect cocks.

My breath caught at the erotic sight and I then gasped as Kenneth's head dipped and his hot mouth latched onto my right nipple.

Have mercy! I was going to enjoy the perks of being a star witness in hiding.

Yes! Yes! Yes!

The End

Spunky Girl Publishing Mini Catalog

Jasmine Black
~Erotica~Without the Romance

~

Here are some more Jasmine Black stories...

Taken by Two Cops
Jasmine Black

TWENTY-FOUR-YEAR-OLD police officer Martina "Marty" Webster gets a fascinating opportunity to go undercover as a lady of the evening in order to catch a criminal. She's thrilled to be partnered with the two older hunky cops she's secretly attracted to. The male officers are going to teach her all she needs to know to carry out her assignment and they're going to leave no holes barred...

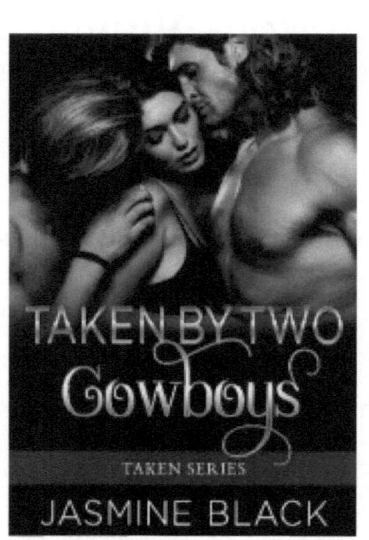

Taken by Two Cowboys
Jasmine Black
Sierra Allan works hard at her late-father's horse ranch. When her step-brother adds her handy girl services to a private auction to help raise money for the failing ranch, she figures there's no harm...but she's stunned when her services are sold to two sexy cowboys who give her an erotic way to save the ranch—submitting to their dark desires..

Taken by Three Billionaires
Jasmine Black
Billionaire friends, Liam, Theo and Elijah have just won Princess
Isabella in a billionaire card game. Isabella knows exactly what the
three men will want from her...she just hadn't expected to have all
three of them at once!

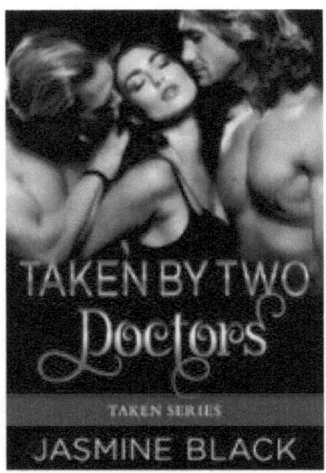

Taken by Two Doctors
A BDSM Medical Fetish Erotica Quickie MFM

Waitress Jean Spelling visits her controversial doctor once a month for some much-needed...stress relief. She looks forward to putting her feet up in the stirrups and enjoys Dr. Ball's naughty unconventional treatments. This time when she arrives, she's surprised to discover that she'll be physically examined by two doctors and they'll prescribe her some much-needed release right there on the examination table!

eBooks in Jasmine Black's Ménage series

eBooks in Jasmine Black's Taken series

Taken by Two X-Husbands
Taken by Two Sugar Daddies
Taken by Two Prison Guards
Taken by Two Elves
Taken by Two Mountain Men
Taken by Two Cops
Taken by Two Santas
Taken by Two Lifeguards
Taken by Two Firefighters
Taken by Two Bikers
Taken by Two Billionaires
Taken by Two Bosses
Taken by Two Cowboys
Taken by Two Personal Trainers
Taken by Two Carpenters

Jasmine Black Website ~ http://www.jasmine-black.com
Twitter ~ @blackerotica1

Taken by Two Mountain Men Excerpt

Jasmine Black

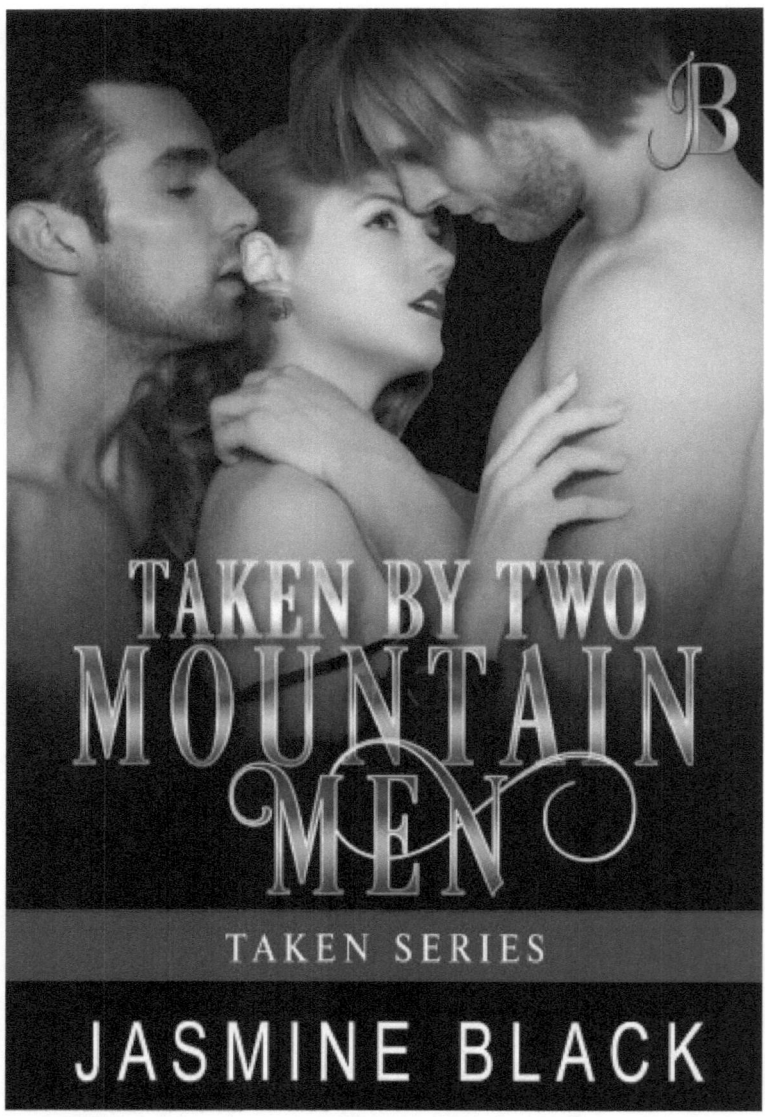

JESSIE BELLE JOHNSTON has always fantasized about being taken by two men but her agoraphobia prevents her from going out and fulfilling her fantasies. Besides, fantasies and reality are two different things...or are they? When the real thing shows up in the form of two hot mountain men at her secluded Canadian Rocky Mountain cabin,

Jessie Belle will find out exactly how it *really feels* like to be taken by two mountain men.

Chapter One

"YOU'RE KIDDING? TROY made a pass at you? I thought those two mountain men were gay?" I asked Chrissy and giggled at the split screen on my computer where my two closest friends, who were identical twins, smiled back at me.

"From the bulges tenting Troy and Bridger's pants after Chrissy politely said she had a boyfriend; they might have been reacting to her hunky boyfriend, whom she'd pointed to at the table where he was waiting on her for her shift to end," my other friend, Megan said and winked.

We all laughed.

The three of us were servers and motel cleaners at the restaurant and adjoining small wilderness motel that Chrissy and Megan's parents owned. The business was on a secluded road, which was an offshoot from the major highway that ran between Banff and Jasper National Parks in the Canadian Rocky Mountains.

The business was isolated and catered to tourists year-round who wanted a remote experience in the Rockies. It was a meeting point for wilderness guides who took their clients into the interior by float plane or interior camping or fishing via canoe on the nearby string of adjoining lakes.

Troy and Bridger stayed at the motel and ate at the restaurant when they came down from their trapping. Sometimes they were gone months on end, living off the land in the mountains, and they'd certainly grown from the gangly pimple-faced teenagers into handsome hunks since I'd seen them several years ago when I'd spent my last summer here at my grandparent's cabin.

I was lucky to have this little stone cabin to live in. It was perched about a half mile up the side of a mountain and a mile from my workplace. So, I walked to and from work and my cabin was rent free, thanks to my grandparents who owned the place and their parents who'd owned it before them.

Unfortunately, I'd had to take a temporary leave from my job because my agoraphobia had returned.

I have an off and on issue of being afraid to leave the safety of wherever I happen to be living at the time my agoraphobia hits. I believe it's thanks to my fighting parents who didn't know any better than to shut up when their three kids were fast asleep. Getting awoken way too many times to high-pitched screaming parents and having things get smashed against the wall on the other side of my bedroom had fried my young nerves. So whenever I got too overtired, my anxiety and subsequent agoraphobia kicked in. Usually I could get it under control before it got too bad, but sometimes, I couldn't.

Complex post traumatic stress disorder was what a shrink had once told me. Well, shit, I could have told him that. He said drugs would help. I tried the drug route but it was too expensive without insurance and I hadn't cared for the side effects, so I'd stopped.

"Hey, are you feeling any better, Jessie Belle? It's been more than a week since you went into seclusion," Chrissy asked, as both my friends expressions grew serious.

"I'm working on it," I lied.

I was still too tense from what had happened to set things off again and didn't venture further than the outhouse or to bathe in a nearby glacial rapids.

"Just keep trying. You've mastered it before and I will keep bringing you groceries until you conquer it again," Meg said with a grin.

She had such confidence in me. I wished I had the same.

"Oh, a reminder," Chrissy broke in, her blue eyes flashing with seriousness. "A bad storm is coming tonight. Your power will most likely go down taking the internet with it. The road up to your place will most likely wash out too, so you might get stranded for a week or two before they fix things. How are you candles and food?"

"My grandparents have lots of candles here and I still have about a month worth of food. You guys are the best, always looking out for me." I replied.

Sure the summer storms scared the crap out of me because the thunder rattled my nerves and reminded me of our noisy abusive household, but this cabin had been in our family for over one hundred years and as Gramps always boasted, no avalanche or landslide had touched it in all that time.

"You're safe there," Chrissy said with a chuckle. "The only other people who use that crazy twisting road are our well-hung gay mountain men."

I laughed, wondering if Chrissy and Megan truly believed those two guys were gay, because they certainly didn't seem that way to me.

"I can come up and get you out before the storm hits. You could stay with Cal and me for as long as you need too," Chrissy offered.

I shook my head as anxiety rushed through me just thinking about leaving the safety of the sturdy stone walls of this cabin and moving in with Chrissy and her new boyfriend.

"I'm fine. Truly," I answered. I would be fine. I'd just pop a sleeping pill. It would relax me.

Both of my friends frowned, probably not believing me.

"Okay. If you change your mind, call before the storm hits. Oh, hey, I hear Cal at the door. Gotta get our supper going. Stay safe, my friend." Chrissy said.

"Bye!" Megan and I called out.

She waved, and then her side of my computer screen went black. Megan was still there, a frown back on her face.

"What's wrong?" I asked as a feeling of unease swept over me.

"I didn't want to say it when Chrissy was here and break her bubble, but those two mountain men are seriously not gay."

I nodded, not feeling in the least bit surprised. I'd never really thought they were into each other, but hey things changed over the years, and they were together in the mountains for extended periods of time. I wouldn't blame them if they had turned to each other for some sexual relief.

"They've made a few passes at me since they've come down from the mountain. I've told them I'm not interested as I have a boyfriend, but they've been asking about you quite a bit," she said.

Surprise hit me.

"Me?"

"Yes. They wanted to know if you have a boyfriend. Where were you? Are you coming back? Stuff like that. But I didn't tell them you are at the cabin. Just that you had a family emergency and had taken a leave of absence. Have they ever made suggestions to you?" Megan asked, a curious expression on her face.

I shrugged.

"The last time they were down, yeah, but I figured they were just playing around. Besides, Chrissy always told me they weren't straight," I admitted.

Megan rolled her eyes and laughed.

"You believed her? Sure, she thinks they are, because that's what our parents tell us, probably to protect us from the rumors."

"Rumors?"

I leaned forward in my chair as fear swept through me.

"They aren't axe murderers, so don't look so worried. Rumor has it they enjoy sharing a woman when they come down from their isolation. With them being up there in the wild, doing that trapping for months on end without female companionship, they get quite horny. When they get back to civilization, they need serious sexual release. I heard that one time they shacked up with a woman for more than a week and all they did twenty-four seven was have sex with her. But you don't have to worry. They're already back in the mountains by now. I heard them talking to dad this afternoon when they came in for lunch. Said they were heading back up tonight to do a bunch of trapping for the overseas market. I figure it will be a couple months before they come back down again."

Mixed emotions sailed through me.

Thankfully, I didn't have to worry about them being killers of people. However I was excited that the two hunky mountain men liked to share a woman after being without sex for so long. I hadn't had sex for quite some time myself, except for some serious masturbating. I'd always fantasized about a threesome, but in reality I knew I would never experience it. It would be too embarrassing.

Megan and I chatted for a while longer before we said our goodnights. Just talking about those two guys though, had gotten me into a hot and horny mood.

It was time to get ready for bed.

A few minutes later, I placed a towel on the floor beneath my feet, undressed at the kitchen sink and began my evening ritual sponge bath.

There was no indoor hot water. Just icy glacial water that came thru a pipe to the tap from a spring on higher ground behind the cabin. While I'd talked with Megan and Chrissy, I'd set a half pot of water to a boil on the stove. Now I placed the steaming pot into the sink and turned on the tap until the water was toasty warm. Then I set the pot on the pine wood counter.

I poured some of that water into the basin and moaned softly as I dipped my hands and washcloth into the refreshingly warm liquid. I soaped the cloth with my planet friendly soap and leisurely massaged my tender nipples and washed along the curves of my plump breasts as I looked out the window at the quiet scenery.

Stunted white bark pine trees grew in abundance at the edge of the yard and up and down the faraway slopes. A few nutcrackers; light gray colored birds with black wings and black beaks, were fluttering around, cracking pinecones and grabbing the seeds inside for food. Golden rays of sunshine illuminated the nearby snow-capped mountains and down below, in the valley, darkness was quickly descending over the lakes and forest as the sun moved behind the mounts. But in the north sky, I spied the dark, threatening clouds of an impending storm. Yup, I would be popping a sleeping pill later for sure.

To my right, perched at the edge of a cliff, the lopsided grey-planked outhouse with the half moon carved into the doorway, stood sentry over the view. I'd already gone to the bathroom before chatting with Chrissy and Megan, so that task was out of the way.

Hurriedly, I soaped the rest of me, rinsed with some fresh water and towel dried. Then I grabbed a glass of ice-cold water from the tap and headed to the bedroom.

Time to masturbate!

Jan Springer ~ Erotic Romance ~

Cowboys For Christmas
Cowboys Online 1 ~ Moose Ranch
Jan Springer
A Canadian Contemporary Ménage Romance m/f/m/m Series

Jennifer Jane (JJ) Watson has spent the past ten Christmases in a maximum-security prison.

The last thing she expects is to get early parole, along with a job on a remote Canadian cattle ranch serving Christmas holiday dinners to three of the sexiest cowboys she's ever met!

Rafe, Brady and Dan thought they were getting a couple of male ex-cons to help out around their secluded ranch, but instead they get an attractive and very appealing female.

In the snowbound wilds of Northern Ontario, female companionship is rare.

It's a good thing the three men like to share...

They're dominating, sexy-as-sin and they fill JJ with the hottest ménage fantasies she's ever had. Suddenly she's craving cowboys for Christmas and wishing for something she knows she can never have...a happily ever after.

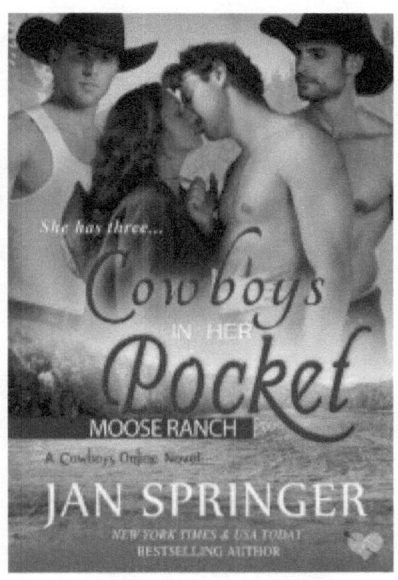

Cowboys In Her Pocket
Cowboys Online 2 ~ Moose Ranch
Jan Springer

*After spending ten years in a maximum-security prison Jennifer Jane (JJ)
Watson got early parole and a job on a remote Canadian cattle ranch
playing housekeeper to three of the sexiest cowboys she's ever met...*

Spring has finally arrived at Moose Ranch, and a single woman fresh
out of prison shouldn't be experiencing scorching ménages with her
three sexy-as-sin cowboys. But JJ's love for her men continues to grow
as she gives into the fevered heat and scorching passions she feels for
each of them.

Life is perfect.

Until her new life is tested when mysterious happenings occur on the
ranch and then one of her cowboys is viciously attacked and injured.

Will JJ's newfound freedom and happiness be ripped away?

Rafe, Brady and Dan never expected to find an attractive and very appealing female to help them out at their secluded ranch. But in the wilds of Northern Ontario, female companionship is rare. It's a good thing the three men like to share...

Brady, Dan and Rafe have never been happier. Their cattle ranch is flourishing and their continued desire to share the sexy woman who cares for them makes their life complete. Until danger threatens to rip everything apart...

Loving Her Cowboys
Cowboys Online 3 ~ Moose Ranch
Jan Springer

AFTER SPENDING TEN years in a maximum-security prison Jennifer Jane (JJ) Watson got early parole and a job on a remote Canadian cattle ranch playing housekeeper to three of the sexiest cowboys she's ever met...

Her love for her cowboys continues to grow as she gives into fevered heat. But JJ's simmering restlessness explodes and she's seriously making up for lost time by pursuing her dreams. There's only one little problem. She hasn't revealed to her bosses what she's been up to while they're away tending to the cattle. She knows when they discover her secret, there will be hell to pay.

Ranchers Rafe, Dan and Brady have found the woman who completes them. She makes their secluded ranch a home-sweet-home. She's vulnerable, sweet and willing to share her bed with all three of them. But when JJ's secret is unwittingly revealed, they're stunned and angry. They figure it's time to dole out some fiery punishment in some mighty naughty ways...

Cowboys In Her Heart
Cowboys Online #4

AFTER SPENDING TEN years in a maximum-security prison, JJ gets unexpected parole and a job on a Canadian ranch serving up scrumptious dinners and lots of hot love to three of the sexiest cowboys she's ever met.

Jennifer Jane "JJ" Watson has never been happier. She's going to have a baby!

Thankfully, their wilderness ranch is a nice distraction for her three sexy cowboys while she's away flying her plane. But when she's home, her dominant hunks are tending to her naughty pregnant cravings and that includes plenty of sizzling ménages.

Rafe, Brady and Dan don't much like the idea of their woman flying the Canadian skies and being at the mercy of the unpredictable Northern Ontario weather. They would prefer having her warming their beds twenty-four seven. But she has a way of getting what she wants and right now she needs her new-found freedom.

Worst fears are realized when JJ, her friend and JJ's plane suddenly go missing and she doesn't come back home to them.

Always Her Cowboys
Cowboys Online 5 ~ Moose Ranch

1

Reader Advisory: Best to read in order. 1. Cowboys for Christmas, 2. Cowboys in Her Pocket, 3. Loving Her Cowboys, 4.Cowboys in Her Heart, 5. Always Her Cowboys. 6. Her Forever Cowboys 7. Claiming Her Cowboys

A Canadian Contemporary Ménage Romance m/f/m/m

JENNIFER JANE (JJ) Watson has spent ten Christmases in a maximum-security prison. The last thing she expected was to get early parole, along with a job on a remote Canadian cattle ranch serving Christmas holiday dinners to three of the sexiest cowboys she's ever met!

Rafe, Brady and Dan thought they were getting male ex-cons to help out around their secluded ranch, but instead they got an attractive and very appealing female. In the snowbound wilds of Northern Ontario, female companionship is rare. It's a good thing the three men like to share...

Christmas is coming once again to Moose Ranch and with JJ's due date approaching, she's distracting herself from anxiety attacks by

1. https://janspringerauthor.files.wordpress.com/2017/11/alwayshercowboys_ebook-1new.jpg

keeping herself ultra-busy preparing for the arrival of her baby and planning Moose Ranch's first annual Christmas party!

In having a wee baby on the way, there's a lot of stress for Brady, Rafe and Dan. Especially due to JJ's decision on having a wilderness mid-wife deliver the baby *at their secluded ranch* - with *all* of them present for the birth! But their concerns don't stop the men from showing JJ how much they love her...out of bed and in!

With wicked snowstorms, a grounded bush plane, a cheerful holiday party and a sweet baby on the way, the owners of Moose Ranch know this will be one sparkling Christmas season they won't soon forget...

PLUS: HER FOREVER COWBOYS ~ Snowy Creek Ranch #1 Cowboys Online #6

Claiming Her Cowboys ~ Moose Ranch #6 Cowboys Online #7

Risqué Girl Delights Boxed Set
(Contemporary Erotic Romance)

2

...a touch of romance, a ménage or both?

Edible Delights

YEARS AGO ALLIE MASTERS lost herself in the scorching passion of a ménage a trois relationship with her two bosses. In order to regain her independence, she walked away.

Max and Nick were very fulfilled with their gorgeous assistant. The lovemaking was breathtaking and both men willingly shared the woman they wanted to spend the rest of their lives with. Then she left.

Now Max and Nick have decided it's time to seduce Allie back into their lives.

Toygasm

IT'S A CASE OF MISTAKEN identity when the two owners of Sexy Toys, show up for an erotic several day photo shoot of their toys with famous nude model Cammie Creek.

---

2. https://janspringerauthor.files.wordpress.com/2015/02/rgdelights_box_js_3d_noshadow-1.jpg

Cammie believes the two hunks are the male models she's supposed to work with. Usually she doesn't mix business with pleasure, but when they're seducing her right there in front of the camera, she can't resist turning them into her own personal naughty toys.

Josh and Jode are enjoying the perks of being male models; hot lust, sizzling toys and the best pleasure they've ever had. But how will Cammie react when she discovers they're actually her bosses and not just male models?

Shy Girl

FINALLY FREE OF AN abusive relationship, "Shy Girl" Emma McCall sheds her inhibitions and explores her sensual side at Club Rendezvous, a club specializing in the Alternate Lifestyle.

At the club she's surprised to find Logan Masters, a sexy hunk she's secretly fantasized about since college. With Logan's help, Emma will experience her ultimate fantasy - a scorching ménage a trois.

Roman and Julietta

HER PERFECT LOVER...

Modern day pirate Julietta Black's life has always been immersed in the violent and traditional ways of piracy. When her family's arch enemy puts a hit out on her family, Julietta knows there's only one way to lift the hit; she must kidnap the enemy's sexy grandson and force a union between the two warring families. Night after night, wrapped in Roman's strong arms, she can't deny the searing attraction blazing between them. Nor can she deny he now holds her heart as well as her life in his hands.

His dream angel...

When Roman Prince's mysterious captor offers him a luscious woman to bed, fierce desire ignites, melting his usually tight self-control. Lust quickly turns to love as he enjoys their naughty trysts more than he should. How will he react when he discovers he's been kidnapped, not for a ransom, but captured for his sperm?

Alpha Outlaws Boxed Set (Books 1-5 Outlaw Lovers)
5 Books!!

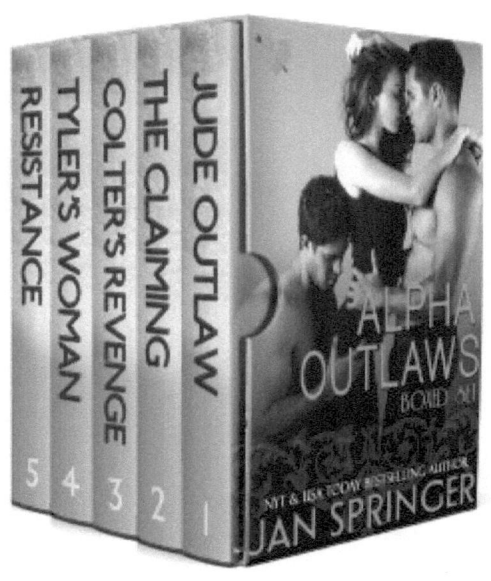

3

IN A WORLD GONE MAD...

A fast-acting virus has killed a majority of the world's female population. With the creation of The Claiming Law, groups of men suddenly have the right to claim a female as their sensual property and the sexy Outlaw brothers are going to declare ownership of the women they love...any way they can.

Jude Outlaw

When Cate Callahan learns Jude is coming home from the Terrorist Wars and is ready to claim her under the new law—with the help of his four brothers—she steals their boat and escapes to the high seas. Unfortunately, her runaway bid for freedom doesn't last long.

Quickly capturing his lover, Jude rekindles the flames and seduces Cate back into his bed.

---

3. https://janspringerauthor.files.wordpress.com/2010/07/alphaoutlaws_js_box_final.jpg

But Jude holds a secret that could make him lose Cate forever...
PLUS
The Claiming
Seeking refuge from the Claiming Law, Callie Callahan hides in a deserted cabin in the Maine woods and is shocked when her ex-flame finds her. She's always craved being in Luke Outlaw's arms. Tasting him. Touching him. Taking him deeply within her. So, what's a girl to do but to delve into the sinful delights he offers.

Luke has finally reunited with the love of his life. He knows there is only one way to keep Callie safe and with him forever. He'll do it with the help of his three brothers and an assortment of naughty toys. Rekindling the flames between them, he unleashes Callie's sensual side, taking her in ways she never dreamed possible, all with the ultimate goal of introducing her to the Outlaw Lovers and The Claiming.

Colter's Revenge
Revenge belongs to Dr. Colter Outlaw when he unexpectedly reunites with the beautiful woman who broke his heart during the Terrorist Wars. Capturing her, collaring her and holding her against her will, he seduces her, fills her with wicked desires and naughty cravings for a delicious ménage. Fully intent on breaking her heart and walking away, Colter's plans unravel when he submits to the carnal pleasures Ashley gives him so freely.

Colter had told her he loved her. He'd whispered promises of rescue from her life as a slave, but when he'd suddenly disappeared, she'd been devastated. Infected with a version of the X-virus that leaves Ashley Blakely sexually excited on a daily basis, she has come to Pleasure Palace to bid on a cure for her illness. She never expected her Outlaw Lover to be there and screw her plans. Nor did she expect to give him her heart and body so easily...

Tyler's Woman
For years Tyler Outlaw and his best friend, Hunter Brown, endured brutal torture and worse in an overseas terrorist prison. Finally, free

of their hell, they return home intent on seducing Laurie into their erotic-filled fantasies.

Laurie Callahan has always experienced red-hot pleasure and passionate love in Tyler Outlaw's arms. But when he's pronounced MIA, presumed dead in the Terrorist Wars, Laurie's world is shattered, and her heart is broken.

Shocked to discover Tyler is alive and he's taken a male lover, Laurie is thrust into a sensual world of sizzling seductions, scorching ménages and the carnal desires that both scarred men crave. But she fears Tyler won't want her when he discovers she's not the same woman he left behind...

****READER CAUTION IS ADVISED (m/m forced scenes) ****

Resistance

In the near future, a virus has been unleashed, killing a majority of the world's female population, forcing the introduction of the Claiming Law. A law that states men have all the rights and women are sexual property claimable by groups of men.

Fugitive female...

Renegade Resistance leader Reena "Red" Wilde is in for the fight of her life when she experiences an erotic attraction to the two most dangerous men she's ever met.

Black ops assassin...

Months ago, Will "Blade" Smith spent one sizzling evening in the arms of a red-haired seductress. Now she's his next assignment. One look into her gorgeous eyes and he's wrestling his heated cravings for her all over again.

Bounty Hunter...

When Cade Outlaw nabs his bounty, sexy-as-sin Reena Wilde, his profession dictates she's hands-off. But he can't ignore the magnetic sparks between them...or that she is the biggest temptation of his life.

Resistance is futile...

After Reena escapes Cade and Will and falls prey to a band of evil hunters, she's grateful her sexy hunks come to her rescue...and in return, saves their lives. Trapped in a solitary cabin during a wicked snowstorm, she can't resist her two, well-hung studs, nor can she deny they've claimed her heart.

Many more Jasmine Black and Jan Springer eBooks, print books, audiobooks plus translated eBooks and print books can be found at http://www.janspringer.com and http://www.jasmine-black.com

Her Forever Cowboys
Excerpt

Jan Springer
Cowboys Online ~ Snowy Creek Ranch #1

SASKADIA WOMEN'S FEDERAL Prison

Saskatchewan, Canada

"You probably have no idea how lucky you are to get accepted into the Freedom Run program, do you?" Milena Allen's parole officer asked as she leaned back in her chair and smiled smugly at Milena.

Blah. Blah. Blah. Tell me something new, or please let me get back to my dishwashing duties.

She'd heard this lecture many times over the past few months. It happened every time the two of them got together to discuss how Milena would integrate back into society through the Freedom Run program...when the time came.

If the time came.

She tensed as Officer Brown prattled on with all the conditions.

Milena's prison release would be dependent on several factors. She needed to stay out of trouble. No fighting with the other inmates. She had to stay physically and mentally healthy. Stay off drugs and no alcohol and keep taking all those prison courses and stay busy with her chores.

Milena sighed inwardly. It appeared as though this meeting would be the same as all the others. She didn't know why she always anticipated good news when she came to this office. She should know by now nothing ever good happened to her. No one on the outside wanted to take a chance on her.

No one wants me.

Milena forced herself to quell her disappointment and focused on a ladybug that crawled across the parole officer's desk.

Huh, ladybugs were said to bring good luck. Too bad she was still incarcerated. She wished she could reach out, pick up the little bug, open a window, and set it free. But she'd learned not to make any sudden moves within the prison system. Unexpected movements got inmates shot dead.

Besides, how could she set it free? All the windows were locked tight. The only way out was the same way it had come in, whatever way that had been.

"Okay, I went out on a limb for you on this one," Officer Brown's voice snapped through Milena's thoughts.

Milena had tuned her out, so she had no idea what the woman was suddenly talking about. She was staring at her, and if Milena didn't know any better, there was a tinge of a genuine smile lifting the woman's thin lips. But then it was gone, leaving Milena with the impression she must have imagined it.

The officer suddenly stood and walked to a nearby closet. She opened the door and dragged out a large dark blue knapsack, and a moment later, she plopped it onto her desk.

Dropped it right on top of the ladybug!

Oh no! Sorry, little bug. Hopefully, you didn't feel any pain.

Milena pushed down the sadness that welled inside her for the fate of the small creature.

"I was able to get this knapsack with the meager funds in the budget for miscellaneous expenses. You'll need it where you're going," the officer said in a condescending tone.

Where am I going? What is happening?

Milena's gaze snapped to the woman's face. If she didn't always have a weird smirk curling her lips, she would have been a nice-looking woman. She had shoulder-length hair the color of strawberries, a dusting of rust-colored freckles across her cheeks, and pretty green eyes.

But that smile she had now...it was a direct contrast to the genuine smile of happiness she'd thought she'd seen moments earlier.

Despite the officer's vulgar expression, a flare of excitement began to uncurl inside Milena.

She was about Milena's age of thirty-two. She had replaced her previous parole officer, Sadie, an older woman that Milena had liked, but Sadie had taken a sudden leave of absence to care for her husband after he'd had a devastating stroke.

Sadie had made it a point to be very personal with the inmates, had truly cared. She'd been the one who'd gotten Milena into the Freedom Run program, and last year, she'd been given a temporary job through Cowboys Online, a program for convicts under the Freedom Run umbrella.

Sadie had always given Milena glimmers of hope that good things would come her way, but she would have to be patient. Most of that hope had died when Sadie left.

This officer wasn't nice. Or reassuring. And she was probably playing a sick twisted game with Milena right now because she still had no idea what the woman was talking about.

"As you know, it would be a conditional parole. Many strings attached. You won't be released into the public like a regular parolee. You might even say you're trading one prison for another. Except this new place has no bars," she said with a chuckle.

Milena's mind whirled. What was she saying?

"Just plenty of trees, very few people. There is a railroad, but it's rarely used. You could try to escape by following it, but it would take you weeks to get out, and by then, the cops would be swarming all over the area, and you wouldn't have a chance. Or the wildlife would kill you before you starved to death in the desolation. You'd either be killed or captured and sent back to a prison somewhere for the rest of your sentence with another ten years tacked on for trying to flee," she paused and stared at Milena with a cold, stern look as if daring her to try an escape.

Milena couldn't stop the shiver of dread rippling down her back. What kind of place where they sending her? It didn't sound pleasant at all.

"The only way in and out of your new home will be a float plane. That's where this knapsack comes in. Suitcases won't get you far in pioneer ranch living. They don't even have electricity or indoor plumbing out there. Talk about off the grid. So yeah, some inconveniences, but hey, you should be used to that after being incarcerated, right? How many years have you been on the inside?" she asked as she drew her attention to her computer screen. The woman knew exactly how many years. She just wanted to rub it in.

Milena stuffed down a flinch and remained quiet.

"Fourteen years plus. You came in at seventeen years old. Young and stupid," the parole officer said. Then she made an odd grunt.

"Some might decide to stay here and forgo the lions, tigers and man-eating bears of the wilderness. But I'm obligated to ask you if you want to go. If so, then sign here and go back to your cell and grab your shit. You could be out of here by nightfall. But think hard before putting pen to paper, Miss Allen. I will give you five minutes to consider what you want to do. Prison is a posh hotel compared to this place. Life on a real working ranch is pretty rough, especially in this case, with this ranch just starting. Only a year old it is. The pay isn't great, but hey, you'll have nowhere to go to spend your money anyways. No stores. No internet access. No nothing. It's a place called Snowy Creek Ranch and located in the Northern Ontario wilderness."

Snowy Creek. Why did that name sound familiar? She'd heard that name before somewhere, hadn't she?

The officer left the knapsack on her desk and then started toward the door.

"I'll be back in a few minutes so you can think. Don't go anywhere," she said with a sarcastic chuckle, and then she left.

Don't go anywhere? Milena shook her head and frowned.

She'd never gotten used to the so-called humorous incarceration remarks that were flung so smoothly around here by the prison personnel and the inmates. She had never liked the authority the guards held over her. The power they used every chance they got in telling her what to do, where to go, and what and when to eat.

Don't go anywhere? Seriously?

Milena rarely swore. Her mother had taught her it was improper for a lady to swear. Inside the prison system, many women did, but she'd always refrained.

Today she'd make an exception.

"Fuck you, bitch," Milena muttered in a low voice.

It felt good to swear. Felt even better to flick her middle finger at the door the parole officer had closed only moments earlier.

And it felt awesome to pick up the pen and sign her name to her release papers.

NORTHERN ONTARIO, CANADA

Ex-convict Milena Allen stared out the passenger window of the floatplane. She studied the scraggly spruce trees, the towering white pines and other coniferous trees that embraced the rocky shorelines of the shimmering blue lakes down below. She still couldn't believe that after fourteen years of being locked up in prison, she was now free.

Well, kind of.

Everything had happened so quickly, just like the parole officer had said.

Only yesterday morning she'd had to make a rash decision. Take the chance at freedom or stay in prison for the rest of her sentence. It was a no-brainer.

She'd accepted the job, packed her meager belongings into the supplied knapsack, and said her goodbyes to the several inmates whom she considered friends. They'd all cried and hugged her, wishing her luck.

There had been many brief moments during her goodbyes when she'd wanted to change her mind and stay with the familiar, but she'd stuffed her fear of leaving prison deep down inside herself and took this chance of a lifetime. Within the hour, she'd been handcuffed and ushered into a prison transfer van.

Twenty-four hours later, she was here.

It was all surreal.

She wished she'd been able to enjoy the scenes of green forests, rock-filled meadows, shimmering lakes, and the late evening, mid-May golden sunshine streaming through the cockpit windows, but uneasiness clambered through her.

Had she made the right decision coming here?

As the sun began to set, it was turning the puffy white clouds into gold, purple, and pink billows and everything below the plane was falling into darkness.

"Touchdown in two minutes. Buckle your seat belt," the lone female pilot said from beside Milena.

Her nervousness increased as she spied a lake looming in the distance.

She nodded jerkily, and the tinge of plane fuel and oil that hung around inside the cockpit suddenly made her stomach tighten with queasiness. She struggled to buckle her seat belt and winced at the clinking sound of foot-long chains on the handcuffs that held her wrists captive to the armrests of the seat.

To be in shackles like this and to be thought of as a troublemaker humiliated her.

The guard who had accompanied her overnight at the hotel and then to the airport had outlined the necessity of shackles on the small floatplane. It was for the safety of the pilot; the guard had explained. Sometimes convicts had the overwhelming urge to try to take over the flight and if something terrible happened like that it wouldn't look good for the programs that helped convicts get early conditional parole.

"That's their dock," the pilot, who was around Milena's age, nodded to the lake.

If she thought Milena could see a dock, she was sorely mistaken. The lake was big, maybe a mile across and two miles long. Everything else looked miniature. The shoreline was rock-lined, and a gloomy black wilderness surrounded the lake.

Goodness, with the sun setting over the land, everything was looking so creepy.

She tensed as doubts dangled over her head like a hangman's noose. This was freaking crazy. She should be happy to be out of prison. She was free. Yet, she was terrified.

As the lake loomed bigger, it appeared midnight black in color and daunting.

Her heart pounded with insane speed as she began to experience visions of the plane crashing into the water and here she was with her hands bound by handcuffs, and she didn't even know how to swim!

Milena closed her eyes and struggled to calm her breaths. She wished Cowboys Online had given her a normal job in a city or a town. Somewhere far away from water. She did not like water. Never had.

She cried out as the plane's pontoons splashed onto the lake, gently rocking the plane. She jerked and cursed beneath her breath as water thumped against the hollow metal floats.

The thunderous roar of the engine had her wanting to plug her ears. Thankfully, the roar quickly turned into a purr and Milena was finally able to relax. A little.

Whew! Safe landing. Everything was good.

Thank you, God! She prayed silently.

A few minutes went by as the plane continued to move.

She kept her eyes closed. The bit of queasiness still clung to her stomach, and she knew without a doubt, she would be sick if she didn't get out into the fresh air and soon.

"We're almost there," the pilot said. There was an underlying tone of amusement to her voice. What had been her name when they'd been introduced back in Thunder Bay? Kay something. Kayley, that was her name.

"I thought you said you weren't afraid of flying?" the pilot suddenly asked.

"I'm not," Milena answered.

She didn't feel like expanding on any details about her fear of water and she was grateful the woman merely grunted.

The plane moved smoothly over the water now and Milena sensed they were slowing.

"I don't see a welcoming committee. Are you sure they know you're coming?" the pilot asked.

She'd said barely five sentences to Milena during the two-hour ride and now she was asking questions?

Milena frowned and opened her eyes. She wished she hadn't.

The dock they were heading toward was too small and too damned close to the creepy water. There were little silver things shooting out of and then splashing back into the water leaving behind rings that rippled outward.

"Fish are jumping tonight. You know what that means?" Kayley asked.

Milena shook her head.

"Fish are hungry and they're looking for mosquitoes for supper. A delicious meal." The pilot laughed. Her eyes were bright and cheerful as she steered the float plane toward the dock.

Milena remembered seeing a similar happiness in her friend, Jennifer Jane Watson, or JJ as everyone called her, when she made a safe landing with her own float plane.

Just thinking of JJ made Milena wish she'd been able to reach out to her friend and let her know she was somewhere in the deep Northern Ontario wilderness just like JJ.

Her old prison friend now had three cowboys to keep her safe, a little baby to love and a rustic ranch house to tend and there had been many a night that Milena had sent up prayers for God to keep her friend and her new family safe.

She'd also dared to say a prayer or two for herself. An appeal asking God if He could see fit that she could be half as lucky as JJ, and He could find a place for her to call home.

A wilderness pioneer existence hadn't been what she'd envisioned but her mother had always told her God works in mysterious ways and she needed to have faith.

"Not sure what to do with you with no one here. Can't bring you back and I'm really running late for my next job."

Kayley was frowning and Milena realized that Kayley could decide to turn the plane around and bring her back to the city.

Heck! There was no way she was going back to prison. She'd prefer starving to death out here if need be.

"I was told by my parole officer that all the information had been sent to them. Maybe he's just running late?"

"He? Which one? There are three of them," the pilot said with a frown as she maneuvered her plane closer to the dock.

Milena's tummy hollowed out.

Three? Why had she had assumed the place was owned by a couple? A man and a woman. Why had she not asked more questions?

"Come to think of it, I wasn't told who would be here. Everything happened so fast," Milena admitted.

The pilot said nothing, and Milena swallowed tightly as the dock drew closer. It was just a few planks of wood for heaven's sake.

Thankfully the sickness in her belly didn't get worse and a moment later the plane nudged against the dock. Luckily it didn't fall apart.

The engine sputtered and then died.

The pilot rushed out of her seat and using the key she'd placed on her keychain, rammed it into the keyhole of Milena's handcuffs. They popped open and fell away. Milena quickly rubbed her sore wrists.

"Sorry, protocol. I would lose my job if I'd let you loose and you hijacked the plane."

"But I don't even know how to fly," Milena burst out with a sudden bout of irritation.

"You'd be surprised how many prisoners learn how to fly using flight simulation programs while in prison."

Darn. Why hadn't she thought of that?

"I could jump you right now and take your plane to Tim buck Two," Milena teased as the pilot placed the cuffs onto a nearby console.

"Hell, girl. You're already here." The pilot winked.

Ouch.

"Listen, they wouldn't send me out here for nothing. So, I am sure your bosses are just running behind. I'm running late myself. And it's getting dark. I can give you my flashlight. Just follow the all-terrain trail that starts at the end of the dock. It'll take you directly to their cabin. It's about a fifteen-minute walk and is near a creek all the way. The trail opens into a huge meadow and that's where you'll find their cabin."

A creek? More water? Shit!

Suddenly Milena had the urge to ask the pilot to get her out of here and bring her back to prison. She was not cut out to work on a horse ranch in the middle of nowhere.

"Here, put some of this on. It's homemade bug spray. Citronella oil, some apple cider vinegar, some witch hazel and some lemon oil. It's your best friend out here during the evening and early morning when the mosquitoes are at their worst," the pilot said as she produced a plastic bottle containing some yellow liquid. Milena watched the pilot spray her own bare arms and dabbed some onto her face. The smell of it was nice. A scent similar to lemon.

"Your turn," she handed the bottle to Milena.

Milena just stared at it, not knowing what to do with it. Crazily she'd never had a spray bottle before.

Kayley must have noticed her hesitation and began showing her parts of the bottle.

"Just press the top button but make sure the spray isn't aimed at your eyes. Here's the hole where the liquid comes out. Keep it away from your face and then just spray any exposed skin. Keep the bottle. Consider it a housewarming gift."

Oh, dear Lord, what kind of a place is this when a bottle of bug spray is considered a housewarming gift?

"Here, take this too. A present from me. I can pick up another one at the airport."

The woman handed Milena a large red plastic flashlight. Then she left the small cockpit and moved quickly down the aisle stopping midway.

A moment later Milena heard the plane door slide open. She twisted in her seat and watched Kayley slip out the open doorway. She'd disappeared so fast, Milena didn't know what to do, so she did nothing.

In prison she'd learned not to make a move until she was told to do so. So, she sat and awaited instructions. She watched the pilot appear on the dock, tie a rope attached to the plane to a metal hitch on a plank.

Through the impending twilight, the pilot suddenly gazed up at Milena, smiled and did motions with her hand signaling Milena to spray herself with the bottle.

Milena nodded. She pointed the hole away from her as she'd been directed and sprayed her arms, back of her hands and her neck. She liked the scent. She just hoped the mosquitoes didn't like it.

When she was finished, she noticed the pilot was now waving at her to come out.

Nervousness zapped through her as she left her seat and on trembling legs headed toward the doorway.

Halfway down the aisle she grabbed her knapsack, lifted the flap, stuffed the spray bottle inside, then slung the knapsack onto her back. With flashlight in hand, she stopped at the entrance of the plane. There was a metal ladder just outside. Below it, she spied the black water moving creepily against the dock, ready to strike, grab and drag her under if she made one wrong move.

Oh my gosh. She did not want to go down this very steep ladder.

"Hey! Are you coming? Daylight is burning!" The pilot's shout made her jump back to reality.

She called this daylight?

Such a good idea coming here, Milena. Real stupid.

She did not dare look around as she descended the ladder and stepped onto the slightly moving pontoon.

Thankfully Kayley was right there. She thrust her hand out and Milena eagerly grabbed it. The pilot must have sensed her uneasiness and awkwardness because she was gentle and slow as she helped Milena onto the dock. Thankfully the planks were solid beneath her feet and a moment later she stepped onto hard ground.

"Come on, I'm not as late as I thought. How about I walk you up a few minutes," the pilot said.

She waved for Milena to follow her. Milena thought it odd that all this protocol of having her restrained and now she was set free. Weird.

Well maybe not so weird. The parole officer had warned her about the wildlife killing her out here.

Milena shivered and quickly followed Kayley. She could barely see as they entered the forest and followed a well-worn path with fresh tread marks. She stumbled several times, but quickly learned to stifle her curses and lift her feet.

"The creek is to your right, past the line of trees about thirty feet away" Kayley said. "Don't wander off this atv trail. If you do, make sure you always go to the right because you'll meet the creek, and it goes right through the meadow where their cabin is located. If you go to your left, you'll get lost in thousands and thousands of desolate acres of forest and meadows."

Lovely.

Now that the lake was out of sight, Milena was noticing shrieking sounds coming from their right side in the woods.

"What are those noises?" she asked in a loud voice so she could be heard above the shrills.

"Frogs. It's mating season in the creek and the mates are calling out to each other."

"My God, how many of them are there? It sounds like a symphony gone out of control."

"Probably thousands. But they're harmless. They do like to eat the mosquitoes, just like the fish do. Do you see the mosquitoes?"

"Yes," Milena answered.

She'd have to be blind not to see them. There were bugs flying right in front of her eyes and she could hear the buzzing as they flew close to her ears. They weren't biting her, but their small bodies were bouncing off her face. It was rather annoying.

"There will be hardly any mosquitoes when you get into the meadow. Oh, and you can turn your flashlight on now. It will help you see," Kayley suggested.

Milena had forgotten about the light held tight in her grip, and she quickly flicked it on. She shone it upon the ground and found it easier to walk. A few minutes later, Kayley stopped.

"Well, this is where I go back. There's still enough light for me so I won't get lost. Just stick to the trail and maybe do a bit of singing. In case."

Milena swallowed as her throat went dry with fear.

"In case?" she croaked.

Kayley shook her head, which sent her straight shoulder length blond hair bouncing around.

"Oh, nothing serious. Just so the animals know you're around. That way they will steer clear of you. Okay, so like it was nice meeting you and I'm sure we'll see each other again sometime."

"Thanks for the bug spray and for the flashlight and for walking in with me for a bit. I really appreciate it. I owe you big time. If there is anything you need, you know where to find me."

That is if she made it to the cabin alive.

"No problem. And don't worry about the guys. They wouldn't hurt a flea."

Guys? Like no other woman was here at this ranch?

Oh great. Just freaking great.

With a wave, Kayley disappeared back down the path they had just come from, and uneasiness wrapped tighter around Milena as she forced herself to keep walking ahead, alone. The strong yellow beam of light gave her just a bit of comfort and she dared not look into the darkness on both sides of her or behind her. The shrieking of frogs grew louder as Milena strolled forward. Man, what a noisy bunch of animals.

To her surprise, the trail was easy to follow with the light. Ankle high ferns hugged the sides of the path and Milena tensed as she spotted little creatures jumping across the trail.

Frogs. Dozens of them. They were hopping this way and that way, and she struggled not to step on one. Other creepy sounds began to sift through the darkening damp air.

Icy shivers scrambled up her spine as a branch snapped somewhere to her left. Fear snapped through her when an owl hooted from almost directly above her.

Oh, God please help me get to safety.

She picked up the pace and pleaded harder.

A few minutes later, the rumble of the plane pierced through the shrieking frogs. The roar of its engines grew louder, and Milena could picture Kayley's floatplane rushing along the surface of the lake in order to gain speed for liftoff.

Gosh, this place was noisier than prison. Who would've thought?

Soon the drone of the plane grew quieter and then it was gone. Kayley had left her here.

Milena's heart sank. She was alone. Totally on her own for the first time in fourteen years.

Is this really happening?

Unwanted emotions overwhelmed her. Tears bubbled up and blinded her. Oh, man, she had not expected to break down the instant she was alone.

Frustration at her sudden lack of control made her sob. She wiped her eyes with the back of her right hand and forced herself forward.

She was crazy. She had to be to come out here to live with strangers. What had she been thinking? What kind of insane person ran Cowboys Online? To allow a woman fresh out of prison to fend for herself in the middle of thousands and thousands of acres of forest and lakes?

What if she ran into a bear?

She remembered encountering a bear last summer during her short work stay at Moose Ranch. Not a pleasant experience at all. Thankfully a stranger had come along and saved her. But it appeared there was no stranger coming to her rescue now.

She swore she heard a growl in the woods to her left.

No!

A second later she was running and then the path suddenly ended, and she burst into a mist enshrouded meadow. She stopped abruptly when she realized there was no more path to follow.

Seriously?

Stay to the right if you get lost, Kayley had said. Or had she said left?

Milena's heart began to thump way too fast. She forced her breathing to slow down. She'd had a panic attack or two over the years and she felt as if she might have one now.

Kind of hard not to have one with the situation she'd been stuck in. Prison did that. Crushed your confidence. Screwed with your head until you felt like a nobody.

Well, she *was* a somebody and she *was* free. Kind of. She just had to make the best of this situation.

She shone the flashlight to her right. In the ankle high wet grass, she noticed a trail. She would follow it.

She stepped forward into the swirling cold mist and stuck to the rutted trail that veered to the right. A few minutes of walking and she stopped short when she spied a log cabin right in front of her.

Here are ways we can connect:

Jasmine Black Website at http://janspringerauthor.wordpress.com/jasmine-black/

Jan Springer Website at http://www.janspringer.com[1]

Instagram – http://www.instagram.com/janspringerauthor

Facebook - https://www.facebook.com/janspringereroticromance

Twitter Jan Springer- https://twitter.com/janspringer @janspringer

Twitter Jasmine Black - https://twitter.com/blackerotica1 @blackerotica1

Pinterest - http://www.pinterest.com/janspringer1/

Jan's Blog - http://janspringerauthor.wordpress.com/blog-2/

Happy Reading,

Jasmine Black / Jan Springer

---

1.   http://www.janspringer.com/

Don't miss out!

Visit the website below and you can sign up to receive emails whenever Jasmine Black publishes a new book. There's no charge and no obligation.

https://books2read.com/r/B-A-GIJD-LLMEC

BOOKS 2 READ

Connecting independent readers to independent writers.